*For JOM*

# Diary of a Teenage Murderer

## **Me**

Dear diary, I appreciate that I didn't do such a great job writing to you last year, so this year one of my resolutions is to write in you as often as I can. Last year I only managed to get to May I seem to remember (and I remember that being a little half arsed too). Given that my only other New Year's resolution is to reduce the immense vastness of my man breasts, I really have no excuses.

A few things about me I suppose is a good place to start (just in case I develop amnesia at some point during the year or have a massive head trauma). My name is Matthew Patterson, I have just turned 16 (12$^{th}$ December) and I am in the last year of my GCSE's (year 11). I go to Kingswood Community College in Worthing (Sussex) and live in Beacon Street (also in Worthing). Bloody hell, that's a lot of brackets! (Might as well go for one more).

I have a younger brother called Oliver who is 7 and generally a pain in the ass - no sisters thank God. My Mum and Dad are Alison and Patrick, my Mum is a hairdresser (she has her own salon about 5 minutes from our house) and my Dad works as an estate agent in Worthing, selling "Overpriced houses to idiots who can't afford them!" to quote the slightly balding, middle aged fella. Mum and dad are generally a pain in the ass too.

I am an average student in school I suppose. I can be a little lazy and only really work when I really have to. I do however enjoy writing poems and short stories, but surprisingly I'm a little bit crap at English, rarely scoring a C grade in exams. Everyone is agreed that I have ability, but the word 'lazy' and Matthew Patterson generally go hand in hand.

I am not particularly sporty or overly active, but I do attend Karate classes once a week, which I think I enjoy. I seem to pick up injuries far too often though, which I definitely do not enjoy. It is a good stress reliever and gets me out of the house, doing something sort of constructive with my life. I have been going for about 3 years now and I think I'm getting pretty good. I gained my brown belt last summer and if all goes well and I can keep the injuries to a minimum I should be able to go for my black belt in around a year and a half.

I'm still a virgin. Not that I am particularly bothered by this, but figured I would share this with you dear diary in the spirit of openness and sharing.

I am however likely to remain a virgin for a fair while as the recent large dose of festive cheer has left me with a distinct cleavage, which I am certain that the female of the species do not find at all attractive.

That's enough about me for now, I'm sure we will get to know each other more as the year goes on.

## **January**

### **Sunday, January 1st**

Its New Year's Day here in sunny Sussex and all is well. I have not had a particularly constructive day. I dug out the old PlayStation from the attic yesterday and pretty much managed about 12 hours of good old fashioned slobbing on it today: Tekken, Tomb Raider and grand theft auto were the main sources of time wasting. Oliver came in and played for about half an hour until mum called him down to go to a friend's house for a 'play date'. I am not too sure that I'm all that happy with him having a better social life than me, the little shit – but he definitely does though. I do have friends, but they involve effort and I don't think I really have it in me at the moment. Far easier to sit on my arse and wiggle my thumbs!

I'm generally quite lazy, but today has been monumentally pathetic, even by my standards. I am sure that it has something to do with the large amount of vodka and gin I consumed last night. My dad had a few of his boring estate agent chums over for New Year and mum had invited a few overly chatty ladies from the salon. Needless to say they all managed to get completely smashed and I sneakily helped myself to copious shots. I can safely conclude that I have now experienced my first hangover. It's a little bit like someone has just removed all of the water from your life and pumped up your brain with sewage so it doesn't quite fit in your skull. Not nice.

Mum made tea at around six o clock, a cooked dinner, well an over cooked dinner to be precise. My mums cooking is shocking! And as the years go by I am certain it is getting worse. Obviously it was Christmas day last week, and she decided that she would do us a family fry up for our festive breakfast. This was the rather unattractive breakfast menu on offer:

Sausages: Charcoal
Bacon: Identifiable only by dental records
Beans: Like little evil orange balls of steel
Tomatoes (I didn't have any!): They looked ok but smelt a little of smoked haddock that was grilled the night before – I'm not a big fan of haddock at the best of times, and certainly not for breakfast.
Eggs: Surprisingly undercooked
Other Matter: I can only describe it as a 'slimy organic mess.' I am assuming it was black pudding, but to be honest it could have been anything – again I opted out

Thankfully my Dad cooked the Christmas dinner, so at least that was semi edible, in comparison to Mum he like the head chef at the Savoy.

I think tomorrow I will leave the house and head into town. I have £165 of Christmas money to spend and there is a second hand Sony PS Vita with my name on it in the Cash Converter shop. It's not so much a second hand shop, but more of a place where stolen goods end up. Poor people or those on drugs, rob stuff and take it there to sell. I bet the poor junkie that took the PS Vita in got about £5 for it and they have it on sale for £85 for the console and a free game.

During the evening, my mum insisted that we all get together in the living room and play some family games. Not the best idea, given how dysfunctional my family are most of the time. The evening progressed as follows:

Charades: started well, mum did a great display of 'The Matrix' (you could definitely tell that she used to be good at gymnastics). Nobody got dads attempt at 'Dirty Dancing', which was basically just him grinding the air in a rather desperate way. Oliver managed to demonstrate a blinding version of 'The Lion King'. Then we had to stop the game, as my mum found my first syllable for Titanic a little too suggestive for a family game. (Tit-an-ic, how else could you do it?). "Let's play another game, before this gets any ruder!" said Mum. Perhaps if I hadn't simulated licking the nipples on my imaginary giant breasts we would have played this game for slightly longer.

Frustration: Frustration basically involves pressing a dice in the centre of a game board and moving your counters around in an attempt to get them safely home. The fun (and arguments, and violence) begins when you land on an opponent and send them back to the start of the board. This becomes particularly irritating when you are just about to get one of your counters safely home, and gets unbearably distressing when everyone gangs up on you. Our relaxed 'family' game ended prematurely with Oliver punching the 'popomatic' dice mechanism into a million pieces, throwing the board across the room while shouting, "I hate this pissing game. What a load of piss!" A superb outburst from the 7 year old, which got him sent straight to bed. Ironically, I was laughing so much that I almost pissed myself.

Trivial Pursuit: Minus Oliver, the 3 of us managed a reasonably civilised game of Trivial Pursuit. A boring game really as there are hardly any ways of effectively cheating.

Monopoly: The best game for cheating and the only game guaranteed to result in a family argument. The game followed the same pattern as the previous 1000 games of monopoly we have played together as a family:

- I wind everyone up by attempting to short-change them during every transaction (which I still think is funny!)
- My Mum (as she is too nice) is reduced to the status of a big issue seller within 10 minutes and gives all of her remaining money and cards to my dad to help him win.
- My Dad attempted to steal property cards on at least 2 occasions.
- At least 1 argument about the rules surrounding getting out of jail, using a 'get out of jail free card' or whether you should

receive rent while in jail. This sometimes reaches a point where my dad says, "Right, where the hell is the rule book! Let's sort this out once and for all!" Needless to say, we have no rule book.
- My dad landing on one of my mega properties and declaring that he is too tired to carry on and that the game is a draw.
- Me, winding my father up about the game (while pulling exceptionally smug faces), to the point where he says things like: "why do you have to be such an asshole about this!", "No. You did not beat me. I decided to stop because you have cheated." Or my particular favourite, "We are never playing this game again until you can learn to play properly." Ahhh, the sweet smell of victory.

What the bloody hell is a 'play date'? Been bugging me all day.

## Monday, January 2nd

Needless to say that I didn't make it into town as I had planned, or leave the house for that matter! Another day wasted, I really have to get out tomorrow. I am now down to £160 as I gave Oliver £5 to get the pair of us some chocolate and Coke Cola for our Tekken marathon on the PlayStation. I have eaten so much chocolate over the last couple of weeks and I think it's starting to show. Luckily I am pretty tall so I do get away with the old Christmas swell better than most. I am usually pretty fit (even if I do say so myself), but certainly not at the moment! I play football (occasionally) for the school and once in a blue moon for a local team. Karate training starts back up a week today, which should help me shed a few pounds. I must try and stretch a bit before then or it really will hurt, I don't think I have actually been since before my birthday, so I am quite prepared to be on the receiving end of a kicking!

I am starting to feel a bit flabby around the sides, I think I will get up at 8:00 am tomorrow and go for a quick mile run.

Maybe even 2.

**Tuesday, January 3rd**

I got up at 11:36 and quite obviously didn't go for a run. To make matters worse I then went downstairs and gorged myself on 3 bacon sandwiches, 2 cups of tea and a bar of chocolate that someone foolishly left in the fridge! My stomach is slightly bigger today and is starting to resemble a beach ball. Not a fully inflated one, but it is well on the way.

I went back to bed with my second cup of tea and took my well-read copy of Red Dwarf with me, I must have reached double figures with how many times I have read it now, it is such a great book! We should be made to study this for English literature not 'To Kill a Mocking Bird' or 'Of Mice and Men', they are good, but this is a classic! Rob Grant and Doug Naylor deserve the Nobel Prize for literature in my opinion (although I'm not sure how 2 people writing a book actually works).

I am not a big reader, but when I do read I tend to stick to funny books. Truth be told I get tired very quickly when I read and fall asleep after just a few pages. Mum suggested that I should have my eyes tested, but I consider this skill to be a bit of a gift.

Mum and Dad were back in work today so I was left with Oliver and thought it best to leave him watching Nickelodeon all day (it's not as if they were bloody paying me). I got up again at around 1 o'clock and stumbled downstairs to join him; I obviously took my duvet with me and fell asleep on the sofa for an hour or so. I am sleeping a lot at the moment; I definitely think that the less you do the more sleep you need. I have struck a deal with Oliver, he makes me a cup of tea and brings me 2 biscuits and I give him £1, a great little system.
When Dad got home he said, "Who the hell has finished all the bacon?" Obviously aimed straight at me. I felt no guilt, how could I? The 3 bacon sandwiches I made were delicious.

When my mum got home, she went straight to the kitchen and said, "Which greedy pig has eaten my chocolate?"

"Oliver!" I shouted, and handed him another pound. Another great system! Had I admitted to eating it I would not have heard the end of it for days. But Oliver would have been instantly forgiven. I think it is simply because they love him more than me.

I have decided to do some sit-ups first thing in the morning, perhaps getting up at 8:30am is going to be a little more realistic.

**Wednesday, January 4th**

I opened my eyes at 9:54am, and laughed at the idea of getting up and doing some sit ups and went straight back to sleep.

Today, I did manage to leave the house!! I wandered into town at around 3pm, not a bad effort really considering just how lazy I have been feeling recently. I also remembered to feed my goldfish, something I am sure I haven't done since Christmas day; people like me shouldn't be entrusted with the lives of other things. It was freezing out today; it probably didn't help that I chose to wear just a t-shirt with a coat over the top. I was so cold that I nearly decided to spend some of my Christmas money on a taxi home from town.

I now have £53 left. I got myself a good deal on the PS Vita, I managed to haggle the console and 3 games for £100 and have been playing it since I got back. The Call of Duty game is a winner, a one man army stomping my way through tons of baddies, blowing shit up and generally kicking ass, life doesn't get any better than that!

Dad cooked curry today. As I said, my Dad is the polar opposite to my mum in the kitchen and his curries in particular are very good. My Mum always complains that they are 'too spicy', but I think she is just pissed off because her cooking can only be defined as being 'dog shit' in comparison.

Oliver spent the whole day peering over my shoulder watching me play my game, occasionally asking "Can I have a go now please Matt?" He never did get to have a go, which I do now while writing this, feel a little guilty about. I may let him have 5 minutes on it tomorrow (obviously in exchange for a couple of rounds of free tea and biscuits).

I managed 10 sit ups before I hopped into bed to write this. I couldn't manage any more than that due to cramp. God I'm unfit!

This must change; I am in danger of dying young. If things don't change it is only a matter of time before small objects start orbiting me.

## Thursday, January 5th

My best friend (only proper friend really) Martin Drew, called me this morning to ask if I fancied popping over his house. I explained that I was home with Oliver and that he would have to come here. He came round and brought his PS Vita with him to link up to mine, I think my PS Vita is faulty as he seems to beat me on everything, his must be run faster.

Martin is a great lad. He always works hard in school, gets good grades, is never in trouble and is as good a friend as you could ask for. He is a parent's wet dream. My parents would trade me for him in a heartbeat! I have known him since we started high school; we started in the same form together and sat next to each other on the first day and have been friends ever since. He only lives around the corner from me, but we went to different primary schools, I saw him around but had never had reason to talk to him until secondary school. Martin lives with his Mum who is a nurse in Worthing hospital; his Dad is a teacher but lives in Brighton now after they divorced last year. Don't quote me, but rumour has it that Martins Dad was having an affair with another teacher in his department (and he is a science teacher, so she must be weird looking! The ones in my school certainly are). Martin seemed to cope pretty well with the whole split situation, he spends most weekends with his dad at his flat in Brighton, they go fishing, go to the movies and bowling – all the kinds of things my father never does with me!

We didn't play the PS Vita for long, I lied that my thumb was aching to stop the humiliation of being constantly beaten.

We spent the rest of the day watching episodes of Red Dwarf and I let Oliver play my PS Vita to make up for being such a sod to him yesterday. I impressively managed to get him to make Martin and I 8 full rounds of tea and biscuits.

Mum got home at about 6:00pm and moaned at me for being bone idle and not doing anything around the house. Martin felt uncomfortable with the constant moaning and made his excuses and left. I decided to Hoover so I wouldn't have to listen to mum and get her off my back at the same time.
Dad got back just as I had finished hoovering and Mum began moaning to him about me, so naturally he started moaning at me too, nice. Oliver never gets moaned at.

To top off a crappy day, Mum cooked. Finder's crispy pancakes (though not so crispy - impressive) with peas and mash. Mash was good to be fair, but I have a dark feeling that I will have to wait until next New Years to 'pass' the indigestible peas I stupidly ate.

I spent the evening practicing on my PS Vita to ensure that next time Martin and I lock cables I am not so dreadful!

11 press ups this evening. I had to stop at 11 as it really felt like I was going to suffer an anal prolapse.

**Friday, January 6th**

Another day out, I have no idea where all this energy has arrived from. I went swimming at the local leisure centre with Martin and felt very fat in my budgie smugglers (Note to self: Buy some swimming trunks that do not show the entire world the precise contours of my nut sack and/or my ass crack – it could not have been a nice sight for the unsuspecting swimmers of Worthing).

As far as my New Year's resolutions go I think I'm doing fairly well. I have written in my diary every day and started to make a small effort with respect to exercising. I am going to have to step it up a little though and do a little more, plus eat less too. We are going on a family holiday to Lanzarote this summer (straight after my last GCSE) and I have no intention of being a fat and pathetically white vast slug on the beach!

When we left the pool we walked past a group of kids from my school sitting on the wall. They were smoking, drinking and swearing very loud on purpose (supposed to be cool I think). The ring leader was Todd Phillips, he is quite a nasty piece of work and is in my year at school (not that he is ever there!). He joined our school last October from Worthing College after being expelled for hitting a teacher – nice kid. I have never heard of anyone being called Todd in this country before, a bit of an American name if you ask me. All he has done at my school is cause misery and hassle wherever he goes, everyone hates him and everyone is afraid of him. As Martin and I walked past he unfortunately noticed and started to hurl abuse our way. "Check out these fucking bum boys! You been swimming together you gay fucks? I'm talking to you, Oi! Fucking don't make me smack you." His mates all laughed and egged him on. As you can tell dear diary, he really does have a way with words, particularly those beginning with F. He is only happy it seems; when he is trying to intimidate others.

Obviously we did our best to ignore him and quickened our pace to get away from the nutter (trying not to look like we were). He must have been too pissed or stoned to have been that offended by us, as all we received was a final torrent of abuse from him "Off home to bum? You pair of twats, wait 'til I catch up with you on Monday!" We will wait until you sober up you fucking idiot!

We weren't really that shaken up by him, just a bit annoyed by the fact that he reminded us that we were back at school again on Monday, gutted. I like to feel I can look after myself when it comes down to it. I do Karate, I'm reasonably fit and quite fast when I need to be, but let's face it, he is a nutter and I really would rather not have to fight him. There is a realistic chance that he carries a knife and could well be stupid enough to go and use it. If I'm honest I do feel very uneasy around him, he is quite unpredictable.

## Saturday, January 7th

I was rudely awoken this morning by my dad who was furious that his paper had not arrived. I have no idea why he can't go down he newsagents himself in his car. I am turning into a bit of a slave in this house. It was bloody cold and pissing down too.

The one benefit of being up at 8:30 on a Saturday is that I get to opt out of my mother's 'fry ups' by quickly filling myself up with toast.

Spent most of today reading Red Dwarf before being literally dragged to my Nan's at 5:00pm. I love my Nan, but she really does smell, and her tea is how I imagine that Satan's piss would taste. For a start she makes it with sterilised milk and secondly she uses leaf tea. I think these items must only be available from a 'Nan shop' I have never seen sterilised milk in any of the shops I go to, maybe my Nan makes it herself, maybe she gets it by….. No no, some things are obviously best left unsaid.

Nan's was painless; I played football with Oliver in the garden, quick peck on the cheek, £1 (no idea how she gets them so warm) pressed into my palm and home.

Counted up my money this evening, I only have £38, I'm sure Oliver is stealing from me!

Woke up at 3:26 am after a worrying dream about a factory of old ladies in cages being 'milked' by my Nan. Chilling.

## Sunday, January 8th

My last day as a free man! Back to school, mock exams, stress, dodging Todd Phillips and worst of all, having to get out of bed at 7:00am.

How better to spend it than by arguing with my family all day. I started well by teasing my brother when he was trying to watch TV by flicking his ears, swapping channels and calling him 'little prince pissy pants'. I am not normally so horrible, but I think it's the stress of having to go back to school (or the fact that the little bastard is stealing my money). I am not proud of calling him 'little prince pissy pants' as this is a bit of a sore spot and a sure fire way of making him cry, he occasionally still wets the bed you see. I will say sorry and buy him something from my money to make peace (providing he hasn't robbed all my money by then, the little shit).

After Oliver had left the room in tears, my father decided that he wanted a full on argument with me. My father instigates most of the arguing in the house with some of the following classic opening gambits:

Why do you bully your brother, do you need help?
Your room is a disgrace!

Why can't you do some school work? Do you want to work as a dustman?
Why do you insist on playing your music so loud?
Why can't you listen to proper music?
Why can't you put your dirty plate/glass in the kitchen when you have finished?
Are you determined to grow up to be a bum/sponge?
Eat your dinner; your mother spent ages cooking that/there are starving people in the word!
Can't you help your mother around the house? You really are a useless waste of space.
Why don't you get out of the house, you have been playing that damn game all day?
For god sake you are 16 years old, have a fucking shower, you smell!

Love the last one. Very dad.

Mum is not one to be left out but has less of a repertoire, hers include:

Can you stop leaving your rubbish around the house?
Can you make an effort to eat that, there are people starving in the world/I spent ages cooking that
Can you stop making your brother cry before I strangle you!

I do seem to aggravate my parents during these little tête a têtes, by doing one of two things:

1) Staying absolutely silent, or my favourite

2) Agreeing with everything that I am accused of, and apologising for all my shortcomings insisting I will change immediately.

For some reason the second retort method seems to drive my parents nuts, so I save it for when I am really board, not to be overused, creates just too much hassle.

Today's argument was pretty run of the mill and did end up with me being sent upstairs for being 'an immature little shit' and 'a sponging useless sod'. My dad brought up the £1 I received from my Nan as a piece of psychological warfare today, saying "I noticed you taking more money from your Nan, she is 78! She has no money as it is without you taking money off her each week. Can't you say no!?"

I believe that it was the following retort that got me sent upstairs on this particular occasion: "It was £1. What exactly am I preventing her from buying by accepting it as a gift and not offending her? More pissy tasting milk?"

I remembered to feed my fish again today; it's not looking too well to be honest, probably due to the fact that it gets fed about once a week! I must remember to feed it a little every day. Just like I must remember to do a few sit ups every day. Who am I kidding, perhaps my dad does have a point, maybe I am a bit of a useless waste of space.

Ha ha, "Pissy tasting milk", I do amuse myself at times.

## Monday, January 9th

Back to school, joy.

As usual Martin knocked the door at 7:55 on the dot, and as usual I left the house at 8:10 ensuring that not only would we have to rush all the way, but also that Martin would be pissed off with me the whole way too.

School was surprisingly pretty painless to be fair, but then I have never really had much of an issue with the act of being 'in school'; I just have an issue with the 'doing' of work. I am, if you haven't already figured out dear diary a bit of a lazy sod at heart. Here is a little break down of the subjects I am studying – in no particular order:

French – I am basically 'Merde!' At this subject and have no interest in it what so ever. That is, apart from the buxom Mdm Jones – who is a mid 40's welsh vixen with a huge bum and what must be a 48DD set of cha cha's. I find something unusually alluring about her. I'm sure she could kill a man between those chest beasts of hers, but I believe that it may just be worth taking the risk. I guess that's why I find her so alluring.

I find French a bit of a pointless subject to be honest. I have been there only once on a school trip while in year 9, and never plan to go back. Despite making a valiant attempt to converse with the natives, my enthusiasm for all things French was well and truly squashed by the utter rudeness of the people I met. Now I appreciate that we only spent half a day in Dieppe, and I only tried to speak to three people: a lady selling ice creams, a Mc Donald's cashier and a man in a sweet shop. At the time I had perfected the French needed to ask for stuff (Je Voudrais or something like that! See I told you, I really am bad at French!), and I asked slowly and clearly, pointing at the exact items I wanted to aid the transaction. All three of them looked at me as it I had dropped my trousers to my ankles, turned around, touched my toes and stuck a finger up my arse.

In summary, French is crap because those 3 French peoples attitude was crap. I'm sure everyone else in the country is lovely.

Science –I am good at this subject, in fact I am certain that I am better than the teacher is (Mr Stevens). I have pretty much had to teach myself the entire syllabus for my GCSE's as he is such a useless fuckwit of a teacher and completely unable to control the class in any way. I obviously don't do anything to help the situation in any way, shape or form with my own behaviour, but I only start talking or messing about because I get so bored waiting for the class to stop talking long enough for him to actually start teaching.

Science lessons always tend to follow the same recipe:

1. Arrive 5 to 10 minutes late

2. Class all have a good chin wag while the teacher repeatedly says "Come on guys, can we please get ourselves ready to work!"
3. Class becomes quiet(ish), teacher starts to introduce the days lesson
4. He is interrupted mid flow by a funny noise or wise crack
5. He stops teaching
6. The class erupts in laughter
7. The teacher says "I will not carry on until you are all quiet and listening".
8. The class revert back to chit chatting.
9. Go back to point number 3 and repeat.

Hence, I have been teaching myself out of a revision guide and have made pretty good progress.

Maths – Hate maths, but I'm ok at it. It looks as if I will get a C or maybe even a B in Maths, and that's with my doing bugger all work. I am considering doing it as an A level next year. The only problem is that I find it incredibly dull. The teacher is fine, the class are well behaved but the work is just so tedious. I have no idea why, if you get something first time, that you have to do a further 38 examples of similar questions from a battered old Maths text book.

PE – love PE, hate Rugby. What a stupid game! I think it is the only game where it helps to be ugly (maybe boxing too). You can never be good at rugby unless you have a complete disregard for your own face. Don't get me wrong, I enjoy watching it on telly (especially the internationals between England

and Wales as my dad claims to be 'part Welsh' – surely something to keep to yourself! But it usually sets up some good banter between us). Martin is in my PE class and he also dislikes Rugby (although he is definitely uglier than me!), so we tend to spend most of our rugby lessons running around to look like we are joining in and avoiding the ball as if it were a lump of rotting monkey dung. The other sports I don't mind, although I am not that great at any of them. Saying that, I did represent the school in a badminton tournament last year. I was knocked out in the first round and had to sit and watch everyone else like a knob for 4 hours, as we were miles away from home.

Geography – Such a bland subject, it is so very easy and so very very dull. The teacher does his best, but I can tell that Mr Jones (who is 110% Welsh and of no relation to the huge melon'd Mdm Jones) is fed up teaching it too. He must be approaching his 60's and spends most of our lessons talking about how fantastic his sons are. They apparently canoe, abseil, run marathons, help rebuild villages in Asia, swim channels and all manner of saintly and energetic deeds. I fucking hate his sons. If I ever meet them, he will be telling his next class about how brilliant their funerals were.

English – I quite like English, but the problem is the English teacher absolutely cannot stand me. I am not altogether sure what I have done to piss her off. Every lesson without fail we clash. It usually starts with her attempting to put me down in some way and ends with my answering back and getting sent out. I think that my English teacher (Miss Millard) speaks to my parents more than I do these days.

ICT – I consider this to be an absolute joke of a subject. Surely ICT is something you use to help you study something else. To be fair, the teacher (Mr Turner) is older than most rocks and knows as much about computers as I do about nuclear physics (not much by the way!). I do feel quite sorry for Mr Turner in all honesty, he really does get bullied quite badly by the vast majority of kids at my school. He is quite an effeminate man and you can only imagine the kind of comments he receives in a modern day comprehensive school. But the cruellest thing is what happens when he turns his back to write on the white board. Paper balls, books, aeroplanes, pens, rubbers, elastic bands. Etc. Etc. You name it, kids threw it at him! Some particularly nasty students (e.g. Todd Phillips) have even taken to spitting at him. I remember one lesson someone nailing the back of his hair with the most foul looking greeny imaginable; it hung there for literally half an hour without him noticing. He did as he always does, nothing, just ignores it. How he manages to continue getting out of bed in the morning is beyond me. Why anyone would want to be a teacher is beyond me.

Music – Why I chose to do this subject is absolute beggars belief! I like listening to music, but I play no instruments and I sing like a dying cat being water boarded. It isn't even funny how bad at this subject I am. Mrs Reeves who teaches it is a bit of a battle axe too. I am pretty sure she too absolutely hates my guts.

Thankfully Todd had taken it upon himself to have another one of his many days off. I doubt he would remember the whole swimming pool meeting; he did seem quite drunk at the time. But he really is an odd lad and only God knows how his mind works, maybe an attempted kicking is indeed on the cards when we next meet.

I was absolutely shattered when I got home today. Not surprising really after spending 2 weeks doing quite literally bugger all! I have just finished watching the first 'Clerks' film. It is an absolutely amazing film. There are only a few films that when I have finished watching them, do I want to just put them straight back on again. Why Kevin smith decided to soil its memory by making the turd filled toilet of a sequel is beyond me. I spoke with Martin online about this and he informed me that a 'Clerks 3' is in the pipeline. Perhaps Mr Smith shares my opinion of his sequel and feels he owes the world a debt. I for one cannot wait to see it.

I am writing this in bed and can't be bothered to get up and feed the fish, my laziness amazes even me at times.

I have just pressed play on Clerks again, nice.

**Tuesday, January 10th**

I was so late this morning that Martin had gone by the time I dragged myself out of my house, can't blame him though, it was particularly cold today.

I have just got back in from Karate and I am having trouble just holding the pen. I have bruises developing everywhere and have pulled my groin (and not in a good way). Bath and bed for me.

I am more of a shower person myself, but you can't beat a bath to soothe aching muscles once in a while. As usual I left a tide mark around the bath and forgot to clean it, my dad dragged me out of my bed (not literally) and made me clean it, saying, "If you don't do it now you will forget and your bloody mother will end up doing it and I will end up with her moaning at me about you." To be fair, he has a point.

Following on from last night's thinking. Here are my top 10 films I will happily watch back to back in the same sitting:

1. Clerks – Awesome!
2. Any of the Star Wars films (even the new ones surprisingly!) – I am a complete Star Wars nerd and can pretty much quote the original 3 films almost word for word. I don't mind the new ones, but would happily stoke the fire that burnt away the mutilated remails of bloody jar jar binks.

3. Any of the Indiana Jones films – I want to be Indiana Jones and I certainly want Sean Connery as my dad too.
4. Dodgeball – I love comedies and this is one of the best.
5. There's something about Mary – I still can't work out how he caught his whole nut in his fly, awesome film.
6. Back to the Future – One the first one! The other 2 are shit!
7. Saving Private Ryan – By this I only mean the first 30 minutes. Absolute carnage! The Germans really did make limb stew on that beach.
8. The Matrix – There are many reasons this film makes my top 10, the main one being the leather covered hot chick. The guns and cool special effects obviously help too.
9. Love actually – I guess I'm a big softy at heart really, but this film absolutely nails it for me and always makes me well up. I think it's the really nice piano music that runs through it that does it.
10. Mary Poppins – God I hope nobody ever reads this list. I don't think I would ever live it down.

Think I will watch 'There's Something About Mary' tonight. Martin once told me that there is a porno called 'There's Something About Mary's Ass'!

Nice.

## Wednesday, January 11<sup>th</sup>

Ah, music today and the lovely Sasha Green! Even though I am utter rubbish at music. I can't sing, play an instrument or even tap along to simplest of rhythms but I absolutely love my music lessons. What I can do really well, is stare lustfully at Sasha's perfectly formed buttocks in her deliberately tight Lycra leggings for an hour solid (literally). She is the reason I chose to do music in the first place and the focus point of most of my dreams, most far too inappropriate to go into here. She sits right in front of me and I just sit there. I just sit there and stare. I just sit there and stare, and drool.

Sasha is about 5' 8", has jet black curly hair that stretches down to her shoulder blades and green jade eyes that pierce right through you. But the best feature she has by miles, is the fact that even though every lad in school (and a high percentage of girls too) adores her, she is unbelievably lovely, genuine and completely down to Earth. One day I will ask her out, but it is not going to be today. Today the image of her Lycra clad buttocks is just about enough. But one day I will man up enough and ask her out, she will probably say no, but maybe, just maybe she might in the slightest of all probabilities just say yes. Oh how I would love to see that bottom minus the Lycra. Wow!

And hopefully one day later in the future, I will cover those round and perfectly formed buttocks in gallon after gallon of oil……..hmmmm. I'm glad dear diary that you do not judge me! Or for that matter, have the ability to read my mind, because at the moment it's absolutely filthy!

## Thursday, January 12th

A dull day today. The only thing of real note was that Todd found his way to school and gave me a dirty look in the science corridor, I looked away. Not worth the grief.

He does try to intimidate me, but it never actually works. I really am not scared of him, which I think annoys him all the more. I am pretty sure that if we did come to blows that I could have him.

I had a very rude dream last night about Sasha, nakedness and oil. It was fantastic!! So much so that I think I will sign off and try hard to have a similar one.

## Friday, January 13th

Well I certainly didn't dream about asses and oil!

What I did dream about however was the following:

- Being trapped in a kind of bottle shaped swimming pool with no way to get to the top and take a breath.

- A large armour plated killing machine that caught me in some kind of trap and started eating me from the feet up.
- Being caught at the top of a skyscraper on fire. If that wasn't enough – it was also populated by flesh eating aliens!

Each of these absolute horrors of dreams woke me up and it took me ages to get back to sleep again. I spent the best part of the day trying to keep my eyes open. I am just about to get into bed and it is only 9:48pm, pathetic really.

## Saturday, January 14th

Thank god for weekends! I stayed in bed until 11:30 today, had some tea and toast and had to wander into town with Oliver so he could have his hair cut. Pretty painless really and I even treated him to a CD from HMV to make up for the whole pissy pants issue last week. For some reason he is into rap at the moment and chose an old snoop doggy dog album. I myself, am not into this kind of music, in fact I despise everything about it and insisted that he went to the counter and paid for it himself (I obviously gave him the money). Sadly my plan was flawed as he is only 7 and the CD he was buying was a parent advisory stickered title, no doubt full of swearing and songs about women with giant asses. So, buy it for him I did. The shame of it.

I also bought myself a game for the PS Vita (not that I have actually played it that much since buying it).

But this is a problem solving game, and I am much more likely to play that (I think).

£15 and a bit of loose change left.


**Sunday, January15th**

The fucking grief that CD has caused is unreal!

I was woken from blissful dreams about Sasha by the lyrics: "So just put your hands way up in the ayer (air) and wave the motherfuckers like you just don't cayer (care), yeaer (yeah)". Apparently my parents heard this too, and were not supportive of my little brother's musical choices.

"You can take this shit straight back to the shops after school on Monday!" was my dad's take on the matter. My mum however decided to take things further; I think the conversation went a bit like this:

Mum: why would you buy him something like that, what were you thinking?

Me: I didn't know it was so bad, besides it was him that wanted it.

Mum: Did you not see the huge sticker on it? What were you thinking?

Me: I was actually trying to do something nice. Do you not get that? I'm not sure I get why I am suddenly in trouble here!

Mum: Well buy him an ice cream then, he is 7 you idiot, not a gangster rapper!

Me: Yes you're right, I really am ever so sorry

Mum: are you trying to be funny?

Me: Not at all, unless, you find my agreeing with you and apologising hilarious?

Mum: you are getting far too mouthy! Don't speak to me like that!

Me: Yes I know, I am sorry, I promise I will change. It is my fault, of course you're right.

Mum: you are grounded, 1 week

Me: I accept my punishment, thank you. I will do my best to change and I am sorry if I am in any way a disappointment to you.

Mum: do you want me to make it 2 weeks?

Me: It's your justice system and I am of course only too happy to support it, but it would not be fair for me to make comment. You must take these kind of decisions yourself I'm afraid.

At this point dad decided to join in and back up his wife.

Dad: Matthew, can you speak properly to your mother and stop being so damn cheeky.

Me: Yes dad, I am sorry; I will of course speak properly to mum. Sorry mum, it won't happen again, I will as I have already promised, try to change. I do so want to be a better boy.

This went on for quite a while and the grand result was my being grounded for 3 weeks and forced to stay in my room for all meals. Suits me, it's what I do most of the time anyway.

I heard Oliver going to bed a few moments ago so thought it best to let him know the grief he had caused. "Look at the shit you got me into you pissy bed little shit", not the most articulate, but I felt it needed saying. His response was beautiful, "Fuck you, anus!" Which to be fair, was a little harsh from a 7 year old (and more than a little worrying), but a great comeback from one so young, fair play. I have now developed a new found love for my little gangster rapping brother! I simply smirked at him and said "Goodnight Ollie."

I have mock GCSE's starting on Tuesday, tomorrow I <u>must</u> revise. I must also find out what exams I have and when they are, god I'm crap sometimes.

"Fuck you, anus!" – Brilliant!

## Monday, January 16th

I finally did some revision today and found out what exams I have. My first one is tomorrow and its French, I am not even bothering to revise for that! My exam on Wednesday is Science so I decided to revise for that instead, I figure at least I have some hope of passing that one. I managed 1 hour 35 minutes (yes I actually timed it) before I got bored and picked up this month's Viz and fell asleep at my desk reading the Fat Slags. My dad woke me up with a rather harsh whack on the head with my science revision guide. He then proceeded to have a good old go at me about how just how lazy I am saying, "Is this what you call revision?" Making sure to throw in a couple of "Do you want to work in a supermarket stacking shelves for a living?" and a few "I wish I was back at school again, you do not know how easy you have it!" for good measure.

Thursday is History, which I'm okish at; 1 hour of blankly looking at a history revision book should just about do it. Geography on Friday morning and Music in the afternoon which is a bit harsh, I didn't think you were supposed to have 2 exams in one day, I'm sure that's against my human rights – so one hour of half arsed revision for Geography and that's this week done. A bit of sitting in my room staring at the wall instead of studying for English and Math's the following week and that's the mocks completed.

I think I have actually mastered the art of 'not revising', I have constructed all manner of games and pastimes that act as the perfect means of sitting at my desk and achieving absolutely nothing, while at the same time convincing my parents that I am doing something of use to keep them off my back.

### Tuesday, January 17th

French exam today, I don't even want to think about it let alone write about it.

I think I cracked a rib at karate tonight, I'm not sure if this continual battering I am receiving is worth it! They do say, "No pain, no gain!" Not too sure I want the gain if it feels like this.

My bath and 2 ibuprofen have had no effect, if this does not improve overnight I do think I will have to go and see the doctor. I haven't bothered telling my parents as they are not the most supportive about my doing Karate at the best of times (which at the moment, this clearly isn't!), they also think I am a bit of a hypochondriac too. So much so that when I cut my finger last year in a Science lesson with a scalpel and was sent home, my dad wouldn't even come and pick me up. I had to walk all the way home with blood literally pissing out of the wound. It was only when he got home and actually saw just how bad it was that he bothered taking me to the hospital. Once there, the doctors quickly revealed that I had indeed cut a tendon in half and needed microsurgery to repair it. Apart from the fact that I had to wear a kind of weird spatula like devise on my hand for a month it healed pretty well.

After that incident I decided to keep all injuries and ailment to myself. Especially the rather embarrassing case of piles I developed after sitting on a cold concrete wall for 4 hours. They don't care, so I don't tell them.

Suppose I had better do a tad of revision before I crash out.


### Wednesday, January 18th

My ribs felt a bit better today; I have been taking ibuprofen all day though. Obviously my dad natural thinks I'm a wimp and my mum thinks I should stop going to Karate altogether. It is lovely to have such supportive parents!

Today pretty much didn't happen. One of those horrid dark and rainy days, when you open the curtains in the morning and it still looks like its midnight outside. I really did feel like having a duvet day today, but it would just have caused more hassle than it's worth.

I went to school, did bugger all and came home.

## Thursday, January 19th

Another dark and bleak day today. School was just as dull and bleak again today, but after school I popped round Martins after school and played on his old PlayStation (yes that's right the first one). He had dug it out of is attic the day before and it was caked in dust and even had a bit of mold growing on it. I was amazed to see that it actually still worked. We played on it for hours and I was so late getting home that I received an almighty bollocking from my Dad, "Where the bloody hell have you been? You are supposed to be grounded! Anything could have happened to you!" Etc etc, you get the point.

I am now grounded for another week. All being well, I should be allowed to go out again when I reach 26.

## Friday, January 20th

These dark winter days really are getting a bit much, it's just so depressing.

I was cheered up slightly on my way to Math's period 5 though. I walked into the Math's block and just happened to glance up the stairwell as I entered. Amy Williams (very cute girl in 6th form!) was walking upstairs in a very short skirt. All I can say is that they were white, lacy and made it very difficult for me to walk up the stairs myself.

Its 10 O clock on a Friday night and I am in bed just about to read a book (Hitchhikers guide to the Galaxy), what a sad and dull life I lead.

Now I'm having trouble trying to get the stairwell image out of my head.

Very white and so very, very lacy.


**Saturday, January 21st**

What a horrible week. I think, I have actually done alright in the mocks considering the utter lack of effort I put in. I will definitely have to put a bit more effort in very soon, as the real exams are not far away. I would like to stay on to 6th form and do some A levels, so I will need to gain at last 5 C grades and above. Not too sure what I will do though, Biology and Chemistry are possibilities but definitely not Physics (Physics is basically math's plus a load of complicated shitty bollocks right?). Math's, English and Geography are the other possibilities, but I don't have a real passion for them. Perhaps I should just get a job. Even if I did get some A levels, I have no idea what I would do with them. I feel another New Year's resolution coming on: Generally sort out my life and develop some aims.

If all that is not bad enough, my goldfish died today. I say today, I suppose technically, he could have died about a week or so ago really and floated there unnoticed. My bedroom has developed a bit of a musky smell over the last week, perhaps that's down to the fishes bloated, floating carcass rotting away. I have sworn to myself never to own a pet again and never to have children. If I can't be trusted to put a pinch of food in a bowl once a day to keep a fish alive I should never be allowed to have kids, no really!

## Sunday, January 22$^{nd}$

All things considered this will have to go down as one of the most unexciting days in history. I did nothing today apart from mope around the house feeling sorry for myself. Outside it was dark and rainy, so indoors I stayed and quite literally did bugger all. Quite often on days like today I enjoy doing a bit of reading, but today I didn't even have the energy to hold a book, much less read it.

Out of the 24 uneventful hours available today, I must have slept or dozed for about 20 of them. Although I did managed to read a little bit more of 'Hitchhikers' - very funny!

## Monday, January 23$^{rd}$

I got into a fight today. Todd was in the corridor with a bunch of his henchmen and a few giggly girls. I had to walk past them on my way to my Math's exam and couldn't really go any other way (and, more to the point why the hell should I). The group went silent as I walked by and I stared dead ahead trying to blank them out of sight and mind. I was concentrating on looking dead ahead and doing by best to shut out the silence so much so that I didn't notice Ryan Meed's (A Todd henchman) foot slide in front of mine. I literally flew. Fair play to Ryan for the trip, it was very skillfully executed. He managed to simultaneously wrap his foot around mine and give me a good shove on the back. Needless to say the corridor erupted with laughter. I lost it. I got up and marched straight at Ryan with a complete red mist, and he was still laughing as I put my fist straight through his nose dropping him to the floor.

I just about saw Todd's fist in the nick of time and managed to get most of my head out of the way. His punch glanced across my bottom lip splitting it slightly. I pulled my right arm back fast and with real venom and let it fly, only for it to be caught by our deputy head Mr. Thomas.

The 3 of us were whisked off to Mr. Thomas's office and to be fair to Ryan he didn't bullshit and came straight out with the truth. He explained that we didn't like each other and that I was rude to them the other day at the swimming pool (I knew they would remember this) and that I had it coming. He went on to explain that his only regret was that he did it on school property. Mr. Thomas seemed to pretty much accept this and then proceeded to lay into Todd (verbally of course). "As for you lad, what a pathetic cowered you are! This wasn't your fight to fight lad. How dare you swing a punch when someone isn't looking, you are a pathetic coward!" This had clearly wound Thomas up and there was definite venom on his tongue, plus I don't think any of the staff liked Todd. Todd had clearly decided that he had had enough of listening to Thomas and walked out of the office, calling out as he left: "I'm not the pathetic one, you sad fat wanker!"

I received a day in the internal exclusion room for my reaction (I suppose I should have said thank you for this in retrospect as I really did hit Ryan pretty hard). Ryan had 2 days external exclusion and a nice fat red nose for instigating the situation. Todd was given a full week external for his 'sad fat wanker' outburst. Nice.

I am still not entirely sure why Todd and his mates hate me so much, it really is an irrational hatred, and I have literally done nothing to have provoked this. I am however reassured that I am not his only target, he is generally pretty nasty to everyone he meets. One thing is for certain though; he really does hate me now! It feels to me that we have now officially locked horns and I don't for a moment expect this to be the end of it. He is going to be on my case more now and will definitely want some kind of retribution for Ryan's nose. He will definitely have it in his head that I have one over him, a worry really as this kid is in a really dark place and I think he is capable of doing something very silly.

Finally got around to giving my ex-goldfish a watery send off this evening. It was definitely him (or her I suppose, just how do you tell??) making my room smell a bit funky!

## Tuesday, January 24th

'The Unit' as the teachers (and detritus of the school) refer to it wasn't that bad but the grief I had from my dad for getting 'thrown in' was. "Why do you want to start acting like all the other useless tossers around here? Their fathers are down the pub all day, and all they do is bugger around on the streets causing trouble. Do you want to be like that? Because I tell you now, if you do you can bloody well do it under someone else's roof, not mine!"

Don't get me wrong; I am not one for getting into trouble often at all. The odd detention for missing homework, or for chatting a little too much in class. I did get in trouble when I was in year 8 for fighting, but it was not that bad, just 2 detentions and a letter home. I was grounded for a month for that, and it wasn't even my fault!!

I was talking to my friends at lunch time eating a mars bar and 3 year 9 boys came over and demanded I hand over my mars bar. I told them to 'fuck off' and licked the mars bar all over with an 'mmmmm' noise to show how nice my chocolate bar was. The roughest looking one (Gary Mason I think his name cowered you are! This wasn't your fight to fight lad. How dare you swing a punch when someone isn't looking, you are a pathetic coward!" This had clearly wound Thomas up and there was definite venom on his tongue, plus I don't think any of the staff liked Todd. Todd had clearly decided that he had had enough of listening to Thomas and walked out of the office, calling out as he left: "I'm not the pathetic one, you sad fat wanker!"

I received a day in the internal exclusion room for my reaction (I suppose I should have said thank you for this in retrospect as I really did hit Ryan pretty hard). Ryan had 2 days external exclusion and a nice fat red nose for instigating the situation. Todd was given a full week external for his 'sad fat wanker' outburst. Nice.

I am still not entirely sure why Todd and his mates hate me so much, it really is an irrational hatred, and I have literally done nothing to have provoked this. I am however reassured that I am not his only target, he is generally pretty nasty to everyone he meets. One thing is for certain though; he really does hate me now! It feels to me that we have now officially locked horns and I don't for a moment expect this to be the end of it. He is going to be on my case more now and will definitely want some kind of retribution for Ryan's nose. He will definitely have it in his head that I have one over him, a worry really as this kid is in a really dark place and I think he is capable of doing something very silly.

Finally got around to giving my ex-goldfish a watery send off this evening. It was definitely him (or her I suppose, just how do you tell??) making my room smell a bit funky!

**Tuesday, January 24th**

'The Unit' as the teachers (and detritus of the school) refer to it wasn't that bad but the grief I had from my dad for getting 'thrown in' was. "Why do you want to start acting like all the other useless tossers around here? Their fathers are down the pub all day, and all they do is bugger around on the streets causing trouble. Do you want to be like that? Because I tell you now, if you do you can bloody well do it under someone else's roof, not mine!"

Don't get me wrong; I am not one for getting into trouble often at all. The odd detention for missing homework, or for chatting a little too much in class. I did get in trouble when I was in year 8 for fighting, but it was not that bad, just 2 detentions and a letter home. I was grounded for a month for that, and it wasn't even my fault!!

I was talking to my friends at lunch time eating a mars bar and 3 year 9 boys came over and demanded I hand over my mars bar. I told them to 'fuck off' and licked the mars bar all over with an 'mmmmm' noise to show how nice my chocolate bar was. The roughest looking one (Gary Mason I think his name was, he was later expelled for bringing a knife into school! Lovely school.) threw a punch at me, which I just managed to step back from. I ran at him and tackled him around the waist knocking him to the floor and threw about 50 punches in 3 seconds before the duty teacher pulled me off - by my hair! (I should have sued).

I remember being spoken to by the Headteacher and him saying "That is a particularly nasty temper you have Matthew! We shall have to keep an eye on you. That boy has had to have 4 stitches in his lip, you had better hope his parents don't tell the police and press charges!" I remember being particularly shaken by that statement. I had heard of those 'young people prisons' and I certainly didn't fancy being sent to one. The thing I remember the most is just how good the rest of that mars bar tasted as I ate it walking home. It had no wrapper, was covered in fluff from my pocket, had a stone embedded in it, but it was the best I have ever had. I think it had the taste of victory on it. I have never had trouble with bullies in school since, until now.

The Headteacher was right however, I do have a pretty bad temper, but I think I keep it pretty much under control. I don't often lose it, and if I do it is because I have been pushed too far. The last time I lost it (apart from the recent fight that is) was about a year ago. My brother slept all night with the light on in his room and apparently it was me that turned it on? This being because I am a 'spiteful older brother' and was trying 'to get him back for pouring water on my bed'. Utter rubbish! It must have been my mother or father forgetting to turn it off in their hurry to plonk themselves back in front of the bloody television.

This argument went on all day and I was forced to stay in my room (in the height of summer!) until I owned up to it. So I smashed up my room. I picked up my trusty hockey stick and started to hit everything. The desk broke in half, the plastic chair shattered, my hifi sparked and smoke came out of it, the walls were on the receiving end of some big dents, the TV was cracked and my wardrobe door ripped off. All this and I still hadn't left the fucking light on in that fucking room!! It still annoys me today. I had to start doing a paper round for this day's work. Not too sure that I ever did get around to paying the whole thing off! The newspaper shop owner also sacked me after 2 months of getting papers mixed up and some days just not bothering to deliver them at all.

Back to normal tomorrow hopefully, the 'Unit' has had the desired effect on me. Being cooped up with a bunch of idiots and a teacher with little if any regard for their own personal hygiene in a very hot and small room is not really my idea of fun. We had to go to break and lunch at different times to everyone else as if we were lepers and started the day earlier and finished later. I don't mind finishing later, but I can really do without the early start! I think we have now fully established the fact that I love my sleep!

Other than being in isolation, today was a pretty dull day. Oh, but I did get kicked in the bollocks at karate, surely nothing is worth that! I really don't think I will go next week, or ever again for that matter.

Halfway through 'Hitchhikers' now and loving it. I wish I could write like that. Maybe I will give it a go one day…..

Who the hell am I kidding; I'm far too lazy!


**Wednesday, January 25$^{th}$**

Results of the mocks today. Far worse than I anticipated! How the hell am I going to worm my way out of this one!? I have hidden the results slip under my mattress while I weigh up my options. The way I see it I have the following 4 choices:

1. Keep very quiet and hope my parents forget I ever did mocks
2. Try to change the grades on my sheet (E's to B's is particularly easy to do so I'm told!)
3. Borrow Martin's result (which to be fair are stupidly good) and cut his name of the top. He doesn't quite do all the same subjects as me, but I don't think my parents really know what I do anyway.
4. Run away to South America.

I am not going to write my results in here, they are far too embarrassing. Plus I can't risk writing them somewhere that may fall into enemy hands. I am really unsure what to do about this one.

I will sleep on it…...literally.

Oh, there is a 5th.

   5. Tell the truth and face the consequences

Ha ha, like that's going to happen!


**Thursday, January 26th**

Today was a first. I was actually waiting outside my front door for Martin to arrive. I have decided that today is the start of great things and that I am officially turning over a new leaf (as clichés go, I kind of like this one).

In school I sat on my own, put my hand up and answered questions, completed all my work and stayed behind at the end of my Chemistry lesson to ask more questions about covalent bonding. I am a reformed character and well on my way to passing these god awful GCSE's.

At home I completed my homework, did some extra Chemistry notes and tidied my desk.

What a great day, I feel almost grown up.

Although I still haven't told my parents about the shocking mock results.

### Friday, January 27th

Woke up at 8:30, completely missed Martin. Got into school late and received a late detention. Todd spotted me in the corridor, threw an egg sandwich at me and called me a wanker, which was nice. I failed to hand in my Chemistry homework and received another detention (I left the fucker on my desk!). I got home and received a bollocking from my mum and dad who had received a phone call from my Head of Year, Mrs. Pearce (twisted and evil woman who is blatantly jealous of youth!!). Old slag wagon Pearce has truly rumbled me and told my parents everything. Report, fights and lateness. I appear to be grounded forever!

What a shit day! Does not really get much worse than this, I will probably die in my sleep to top it all off. It's amazing what difference a day makes.

### Saturday, January 28th

Today was hell. I am basically being held prisoner in my own home. Fair enough, I have been very slack and not done a great deal of work this year, but truthfully I was going to.

Who am I kidding; I can't even lie to myself! I tried to change and failed, so this is probably for the best. Sucks though. My dad has taken all my mod cons out of my room. No TV, no hifi, no PS Vita, no nothing – if it's fun, he took it. I asked him, "Do you want to take my soul as well?" He shot me a cruel look and said, "If you do not pass these exams you are out of my house!"

Fuck, I think he meant that.

I consoled myself by going to bed early and finishing off 'Hitchhikers'. It really has to be up there with my favorite books of all time now. Perhaps I will have a go at writing something, maybe when the exams are over.

### Sunday, January 29th

Day two of prison. Basically sat at my desk for 10 hours today trying to balance things on other things. Rulers on rubbers. Rubbers on rulers. Rulers on my nose. Rulers on rubbers on my nose. God I am bored, and my ass is killing from sitting so much. This is only January I have another 4 ½ months of this bullshit.

I am thinking of starting to mark the days off on my bedroom wall like in prison, but I would probably get grounded through the summer too.

I am even thinking of getting another goldfish as a partner to share in my misery.

I can safely say that this has been the longest and shittest weekend I have ever had. I have just climbed into bed with my copy of Viz; let's just hope that goes some way to cheer me up, God knows I need it.

### Monday, January 30th

I have never looked forward to school so much in my life. It was like being freed after a 20-year jail sentence! I walked into school with Martin not saying a word, just savoring the cold morning air and the taste of freedom.

I spent most of my lessons today with a smug grin on my face staring absently out of the window. Teachers pretty much left me to it and I did very little work all day.

I got home late after a very casual walk. I usually cut through the lanes on my way home, but opted to take the long way home today, over a playing field and through the park enjoying every step of way. Today was a cold but bright winters day and I was savoring every moment of it. My father was home early and gave me grief about being late and pretty much escorted me to my room to ensure I started my revision.

It is a bit difficult to be 'forced' to revise, so instead I spent the evening firing paper balls into the bin and constructing a stationary bow and arrow set from a pencil and elastic band. I fashioned an arrow from a pin from my notice board and a paper clip with a feather made from some paper stuck on with blue tack I scrapped from behind my John Lennon poster. I did no work whatsoever, more out of defiance than anything else to be fair. The bow and arrow was a complete success however.

**Tuesday, January 31st**

Ahhh, the sweet smell of freedom!

Again Martin was amazed to see me waiting for him at the front door. We actually spoke on the way into school, which was a bit weird for us; we usually stomp to school in a kind of miserable silence. Martin wanted to know what I was thinking of doing next year, he was thinking of going to a 6th form college in Brighton and wondered if I was too. I explained that my head wasn't really tuned to studying and I didn't think that I would be able to cope and didn't really know what to do. Martin said, "You are one of the brightest in our year group, but you are just so lazy. If you just did just a bit of work

I think you would be surprised by what you could do."

In all my years at school and countless bollockings from my teachers and parents, no one has ever got through before, but Martin hit a nerve this morning. I decided that I would give things a proper go from tonight and use the time of imprisonment to get back on track.

I was as good as my word tonight, but instead of a little I did a lot. Science postcard notes, history mind maps and even a bit of music theory. I did surprise myself a little in all honesty; it does feel good to be good.

I wasn't allowed to go to karate tonight, probably not such a bad thing considering the regular beatings I seem to be receiving! I did have a quick chat with dad when I popped down to get a cup of tea and explained that I was actually doing some work this evening and that I was starting to consider doing A levels next year, although I didn't know which ones just yet. "Good" he said, "That sounds good."

•

# February

## Wednesday, February 1st

Nice to see the back of January, not a great month, here's hoping that February is a lot better.

I managed another good evening of work tonight. I rewrote a load of geography notes and a few more science postcards. I picked up a French revision guide from the library today and made a start on that too.

My dad made a couple of sneak appearances in my room and said how pleased he was that I was finally taking things seriously.

"At least you have moved on from flicking paper balls!" He winked and passed me a cup of tea.

I think that Sasha has been working out. That ass of hers was looking so tight that I could have opened a beer bottle on it. I am seriously thinking of asking her out, probably best to do it just before half term as if I get shot down at least I have a week away from school to deal with the shame! Plus, being grounded as I am, I can't offer the girl an awful lot at the moment. But this new me with new found direction seems to have also acquired a bit of new found confidence from somewhere and, if ever I was going to do this, now the time. Who was it that said 'Seize the day'? Well they were right and by seizing the day I also hope to 'seize the ass'!

I don't know why, but all of a sudden I really fancy a beer. I don't even like beer.

**Thursday, February 2nd**

I have decided to get myself into shape for when I ask Sasha out. I am not in particularly bad shape, generally quite trim and fit (ish). But I do have a little bit of a belly and there are definite love handles beginning to form. I went for a 2-mile run (17 minutes – not too bad for a first run in quite a while), 30 press ups (I do 20 every Tuesday in karate but have never been good at these) and 50 sit-ups.

Tomorrow I must ask a PE teacher for an exercise to get rid of love handles.

Another productive evening of study too. This postcard system of rewriting notes really seems to be working well for Science and I am getting through the revision guide at quite a rapid pace. I am beginning to think that at least one science next year might be a good idea, probably Biology.

**Friday, February 3rd**

This has to be the first week I have ever been on time to school every day. My form tutor Mr. Harris also pointed out this fact to me, saying "I have noticed a change in your attitude recently, I really hope it continues." That's some pretty good motivation for a lazy sod like me. With my form tutor and dad noticing I'm making an effort I am confident that I can keep this new found determination to improve going.

My dad let me go around Martins this evening as a reward for working so hard this week, things are going alright at home the moment. Martin and I watched a bunch of Scrubs episodes and then a bit of Bill Hicks stand up. I had never even heard of that guy before, but that has to be the funniest thing I have ever seen! I struggled to breathe at times and really thought I was going to pass out. Martin told me that he died a good few years ago from pancreatic cancer, no justice in this world – especially considering that all of the spice girls are still alive.

I spoke to Mr. Partridge (ex-army PE bloke) about my love handles. His response was quite typical of PE teachers in my school.
"If you stopped being such a lazy little toe rag in PE lessons then you wouldn't have bloody love handles, or that 36 DD chest you are growing Pamela!"

Lovely, now I have a big pair of tits.

## Saturday, February 4th

I stayed in and worked this morning (yes, the morning! And yes a Saturday). I figured it would be wise to keep on top of things and stay in dads good books.

In the afternoon we went over to see Nan for a cup of Satan's piss, a hairy kiss and a warm smelly pound. I spent most of the time we were there looking at photos of my granddad. He died while I was a baby so I never really got to meet him, well not that I can remember anyway. He had a big stroke and never recovered from it. I find it weird looking at photos of people who have died. The idea that an image captures a moment of life forever is very odd. I thought about the body too, what does his body look like now, bit grim I know.

My Nan saw me looking at the photo and said:

"You would have loved that man. Fair enough he was a moody old sod at times, but he was a lovely man at heart. He loved you you know; only held you a few times he did. But thought the world of you he did. I miss him."

I really do wish I had known him, seems very unfair that people have to die. I should see more of my Nan.

I managed 30 press ups before I went to bed tonight. I have been touching my man breasts all day, that fucking PE teacher has given me a complex.

I listened to The Smith's on my iPod when I was laying in bed. The whole 'death of my grandfather' had really gotten to me this afternoon and I wanted to think about it a little more. I listened to 'Cemetery Gates' in particular about 10 times in a row. It really does sum up the futility of life and death so well. And in 2 minutes 42 seconds too, utter genius.

"So we go inside and we gravely read the stones, all those people all those lives where are they now? With loves and hate and passions just like mine, they were born and then lived and then they died. Seems so unfair, I want to cry."

Me too Mozza, me too.

### Sunday, February 5th

I worked all day today, it helped that it was raining and cold outside, a really shitty day. I am hammering through the French guide, I must have sort of listened in class as there really is a lot I remember, and that's encouraging. I have almost finished doing my Science postcards and History mind maps. I might even tackle a bit of English literature tomorrow.

## Monday, February 6th

I ate my lunch with Sasha today and have decided that I am definitely going to ask her out this week, it is just a case of when. We break up on Friday, so that's the logical choice. But we do have music together on Wednesday so that's another option. I will sleep on it and decide tomorrow.

It is hard to eat when you are sitting with a girl that you really fancy. Luckily I bring own sandwiches from home, which are a lot easier to eat in front of 'fanciable' girls than a plate of nasty food from the diner. Unluckily however, my Mum decided in her infinite wisdom that today my sandwiches would consist of crab paste. Now don't get me wrong, I am of course in no position to argue, given that I do not actually make the sandwiches myself! But crab paste? It just looks and smells all kind of wrong. How does something like that even get invented? 'I know what this World needs, a bunch of crabs smashed up and boiled into a stinking pink paste that smells like the urinals in Worthing Town Square.'

Needless to say I didn't eat the sandwiches, they stayed safely out of 'nose shot' in my lunch box. I opted instead to just have my Dairy Lee dunkers and apple. The dunkers in particular were a great call. Unbeknownst to me, I managed to leave a little of the cheese matter from the dunkers on my top lip. Sasha pointed, laughed and then reached over and wiped it off with her thumb. She then looked me straight in

the eyes (kind of menacingly really) and put her thumb in her mouth.
It's definitely on!

35 press ups and a bit more tension already in my flaccid man bangers.


**Tuesday, February 7th**

I have decided that I am actually going to ask Sasha out tomorrow instead, I don't think I can wait until Friday. I mean, what if someone else asked her out before me? How devastating would that be? It actually gives me butterflies thinking about doing it, it has been about six months since I last asked a girl out. The recipient on that occasion was a girl called Sammy Grange. Sammy Grange is just stunning, long blonde hair, thin, tall with sparkling blue eyes. She is one of those girls who is destined to either be a supermodel, or married to a footballer/billionaire. She said no. Well, she is a bit of a slag I suppose.

It could well be a no again that I get tomorrow and I need to prepare myself for that, but the rewards of a yes are more than worth it!

So, just how do I describe Sasha to you?

Well as I have said before, jet black curly hair and an amazing ass is a great place to start. I think her mum is Spanish or Greek or something, as she has that sort of olive unblemished skin that pure English girls unfortunately just do not have certainly not the ones from Worthing anyway, that's for sure. Greeny brown eyes, full red lips that need no lipstick and chunky yet slim legs that are to die for. She has this way of biting her bottom lip when she concentrates and has a slight frown that makes all sorts of dirty thoughts flow around my head.

She is just so down to Earth though, and amazingly good looking girl without all the baggage that they usually bring with them. Not overly into her looks, not a bitch, not a slag, just perfect. She does not seem to get a lot of male attention really, I guess that's because most blokes go for the easy win. Sasha is very smart and perhaps it's that intellectual side of her that maybe intimidates most fellas. Not me though!

So, tomorrow is the big day. I have decided that during the last 5 minutes of Music (incidentally just before lunch, so I can run off and burst into flames somewhere if it's a no) I will make my move.

I could only manage 31 press ups tonight and I now have a twitching nipple, surely that's not good!

**Wednesday, February 8th**

This is officially my favorite day ever. Future generations of poets and song writers will identify today as that when the truest of true loves began. I'm officially in love. I have had a few girlfriends in the past but none of this caliber, nowhere near in fact.

My love life to date:

- Naomi Davis – She was my first ever girlfriend. We got together during a disco night put on in our local church hall. My friend at primary school, David asked Naomi if she would go out with me and I asked her friend Michelle is she would go out with David. Naomi said yes via Michelle (score) and Michelle said no via Naomi. Our relationship lasted about 5 slow songs at the end of the disco and 1 clumsy first kiss to 'many rivers to cross' by UB40 (which was an old song even in those days!). David spent that time crying in a chair after being rejected, we ceased being friends from that point on. I see him around occasionally (he now goes to a different secondary school) and I'm sure he still hates me! Naomi is in my Geography and English classes, really nice girl – great choice for a first kiss.

- Suzy Frownes – Another primary school conquest. We got it together after she ticked the yes box on my 'proposal note'. Our relationship lasted all of 3 days. No kissing this time, only holding hands on the menu. She dumped me for a kid 2 years higher than us both, what a trollop. Not seen her since primary school, I think she may have moved.

- Amy Stevens – Amy asked me out in my first year of secondary school. We had no dates but we did manage to have 3 kisses in the 2 weeks we went out for. Amy's was the first tongue I ever touched with my tongue (not counting the tongue sandwiches my Nan insists on forcing us to eat of course). I dumped her when I heard the rumour that she was thinking of dumping me. Amy was in my school but left in year 10 to have a baby. No one has any idea who the father is, mainly due to the fact that she was the biggest bike in our schools history.

- Denise Singer – the schools other bike, unfortunately I didn't get a ride, but I did have a right good go on her horns! I went out with Denise for 2 Tuesday nights in a row at our school youth club. We pretty much spent both of those days behind the youth wing sucking each other's faces off. The second week she grabbed my right hand and put it on her small but perfectly formed left breast. I had to pull my groin away from her to prevent drilling a small hole in her stomach. I squeezed and groped and then went inside the shirt. I just got to pinch her nipples twice before we were disturbed by a youth worker. The following Tuesday she dumped me and was rumored to be 'going out' with that pervey fucking youth worker!

- Michelle Ellins – my last girlfriend to date. We broke up last summer holidays after the most boring 4 month relationship I have ever had and will ever have. Don't get me wrong Michelle is stunning. Model standard beauty, rubber plant standard personality. We went to the cinema to watch King Kong and must have spoken about three sentences each during the whole date, it was like pulling teeth. "What did you think of the film?" was one of mine. "It was alright." Was one of hers….. Classic. So why dear diary did it last so long. Well, truth be told I think we kind of forgot we were actually still going out with each other. One phone call in late July and I was released from her lifeless clutches.

I plonked myself down next to Sasha in music and decided to hit her with a joke I heard on the radio in the shower that morning "My mate has started drinking brake fluid." I said. "What on Earth are you on about Matt?" she smiled.
"He says that he can stop whenever he wants!" She frowned in her cute way and then laughed so loud that the usually meek and quite Mrs. Reeves shouted at us, "Can you two idiots stop messing around and get on with your work!" this made us laugh even more.

Last 5 minutes arrived and I felt no nerves at all, like I said before I had nothing to lose. "Sasha, would you go out with me?" I boldly asked.
"Like boyfriend and girlfriend?" she slyly smiled.
"Exactly!" I said too loudly and ol' Reevesy shot me a dirty look.
"I have been waiting for you to ask for ages." She smiled

I have a great new girlfriend; life is sometimes nice after all.

No need for press ups ever again; women obviously love my ample bosoms.

### Thursday, February 9th

I love mornings; don't know why I haven't noticed how good mornings can be before. I think that there are a load of brand new birds nest have been set up in the trees outside my bedroom window overnight. I have never heard birds singing around here before.

I walked to school with Martin and told him my amazing news; he clearly didn't believe me though! The cheeky bastard said, "Nice one, you could never get a girl like that! In fact if you ever do I will saw off my cock and throw it in the sea!"

When we arrived at school Sasha was waiting for me at the gates on her own, she ran up held my hand and kissed me on the cheek.

"Fancy walking down to the beach after school?" I asked Sasha loudly.
"What for?" she replied
"Martin has something he really needs to do." I said

I really am on cloud 9 at the moment, everything just feels so natural. A few of Sasha's friends were quite complimentary about us as a new couple saying some of the following: 'aren't they cute together', 'it's like they have been together for ages', 'they just really fit' and 'you guys really are the best looking couple in school'.

They were of course right. We do look amazing together, not that I'm particularly handsome or anything! We just look right and really comfortable around each other. When I was dating Michelle, it took 2 weeks before we held hands in public and never in school, it just never felt right. This does.


**Friday, February 10th**

Last day of school today, well for a week at least. I am not too sure whether this is a good or bad thing. I am of course happy to be away from school, but a little worried that I may not see Sasha for a whole week and that would be a nightmare. We exchanged phone numbers today, she gave me her mobile, and I gave her my home number. That is lame! I really must be one of the only kids in school not to have a mobile phone, I must get this sorted. There are kids in year 7 who have brand new iPhones and I have buggar all.

I think I will ring Sasha tomorrow and try and arrange our first proper date, but what can we do? I will have to sleep on that.

I walked Sasha home after school today and we had our first 'proper' kiss. Kisses until this point were kind of….. pecks. Little demonstrations of affection. This was very different! When we got to her front door she span in front of me and grabbed me by the neck with her right hand and pulling me into her so fast I almost developed whiplash. The kiss was amazing, so passionate and tender. I have never experienced anything like it. My toes crunched up, the hairs on the back of my neck stood up, little electrical waves shot down my spine and I got a boner.

### Saturday, February 11th

Its Saturday morning as I'm writing this, I am going to ring Sasha a little later and have settled upon the following options for our first 'Hot Date':

- Bowling – I am shit at bowling, not sure if that is a good or bad thing! On one hand, at least Sasha would win and feel good about herself. But on the other hand, I could look an absolute bell end when I insist upon having the bouncy side rails in place.

- Cinema – an absolute load of bollocks on in the cinemas around here, but a good option is a screening of Clerks in Leicester Square. Only problem with this idea is that the screening is tomorrow and I don't have much money left from Christmas. £18 to be precise. I will suggest it anyway and beg for cash from the folks if I need too! Being my favorite film of all time and pretty much knowing all the words from start to finish may be a bad thing though; I don't want to come across as too geeky.

- A walk in the park – this is not a great option, I have just included it as it may be something Sasha may find romantic. In reality, there are loads of kids from school who will be hanging around the local parks and what the hell would we talk about. The real bonus of simply going for a walk is that it is free. However it is February and the weather outside is dreadful, it is 10:14am as I write and it looks as if it's approaching midnight outside.

- Skiing – I have never actually been 'proper' skiing, but there is a dry slope not too far from here. I have only been once before and let's just say that it wasn't the most positive of experiences. I couldn't quite work out how to use the button lifts and after causing huge queues by constantly falling off them spent the day walking up a massive hill in 30 minutes and the whizzing down in 30 seconds, not the most fun I have ever had. I got the hang of it eventually however and became a little too over confident. On my last attempt I decided to 'try out' a 360 degree turn (having witnessed a competent skier do it earlier in the day). Needless to say, the attempt didn't quite go according to plan. After gathering what can only be described as an 'astonishing' amount of speed on the way down I built up the courage to take on the said trick. All was going well until I reached the ¾ mark. During my daredevil anticlockwise spin, the tip of my left ski touched the surface a little too early. The ski fell off and over I went, I shot into the air for what appeared to be an hour and came crashing down on my side. I proceeded to roll, slide and roll some more all the way to the bottom of the slope. I was literally covered in friction burns! My brand new Levi 501's that my mum had bought for me after much hassling were ruined (this got me in a whole World of trouble) and my pride even damaged even more so. I even managed to get a friction burn on the tip of my nose and on one of my testicles. Perhaps skiing is not the greatest of ideas….

When you think about it there really isn't an awful lot for young couples to do.

Well, I have spoken to Sasha and she has chosen the Clerks option, what a girl! Is time to start working on the parents to tap them up for some cash, I will start with tidying my room, about 3 hours' worth of work I'd say. I will then make a start doing a few jobs around the house, the washing up is pretty straight forward and I may even hoover the lounge too. Then later this evening, when my parents have digested all my hard work I will hit them with my demands.

**Sunday, February 12$^{th}$**

It was my first date with Sasha today and it really could not have gone any better.

Yesterday evening went really well, I completed, Mission: Tidy up the bedroom. It did in fact, take 3 hours and was pretty grim. I had just no idea just how filthy my room was. My mum bangs on about it all the time, "It's disgusting in there!" "How can you live like that!" and "can you please keep that door shut I can't bear the smell or shame!"

Under the bed was by far the worst part of the job, finger/toenail clippings, crisps, 2 old mugs growing new life forms, half of a cheese sandwich, many socks, suspicious tissues and a dead mouse. The mouse really made me jump and it just goes to clarify what a state the room had gotten into, not even rodents can survive in it.

Washing up – check
Hoovering – check
Ironing my school uniform – check
Mugging my dad for £20 – check! (Not such a bad bloke at times!)

I met Sasha at the train station and we kissed. A natural kiss, no pressure, no nerves just a simple yet meaningful kiss. A kiss that just held enough in time to matter – an elongated peck with a dash of passion. Ok, I'm overdoing the kiss now. But it was amazing.

We had decided yesterday that we would head up to London and watch a screening of Clerks at the 'Prince of Wales' cinema in Leicester square. I have been to this cinema before and it is one of my favorite places. It is a really old place that I think closed down years ago, but has been reopened as a sort of 'retro' cinema experience. They don't show new movies at all, but instead show all manner of classics. To give you an idea of what it is like here is the listing for last week:

*Monday, 6$^{th}$ Feb*

Am: Sing-along-a-sound-a-music – Is it wrong that I really like the sound of this?

Pm: Reservoir dogs – Great film! I especially like the high impact poster advertising this classic: "A man, A gun, A blood splat!" Would have been a far better advertising slogan though in my opinion. They opted for the rather tame "Let's go to work."

*Tuesday, 7th Feb*

Am: An Officer and a Gentleman – I watched this about a year ago with my mum. Great film, although ever so slightly spoilt by my mum blubbing all the way through it.
Pm: Citizen Kane – Apparently one of the, if not the best film ever made. I have added its viewing to my mental 'to do' list.

*Wednesday 8th Feb*

Am: Mary Poppins – I love this film, surprised not to see it listed as one of those sing-a-long-a types!
Pm: All's quiet on the western front –never seen it, pretty sure it's a war flick though.

*Thursday 9th Feb*

Am: Casablanca – never seen, not even slightly interested (some kind of famous lovey dovey film I think, not really my cup of tea).
Pm: The Blair Witch Project – A lot of people dislike this film, but I love it. I remember watching it one evening at Martins house when I was in year 10. I am not sure what terrified me more, the film or the short walk home at 11pm?

*Friday 10th Feb*

All Day (starting at 11am): The Matrix Trilogy – Love the first film, cannot stand the others.

*Saturday 11th Feb*

Am: The Lion King 3D – Really? 3D? I thought it was crap in 2D, but they seem to have managed to add a whole new dimension of crap, very clever of them.
Pm: One flew over the cuckoo's nest – a big fat slice of cinematic brilliance!

*Sunday 12th Feb*

Am: Clerks – This is our showing.
Pm: Sing-a-long-a-Rocky Horry Picture Show – I must make sure we leave the building as soon as the film finishes to avoid the bunch of weirdoes that this film seems to attract. I watched the first 10 minutes of it a few months back at Martins house and was not impressed.

We caught the 9.32 train from Worthing station, changed at Brighton for the London train and jumped on the tube at Victoria. The train was great, we sat huddled together my arm around her shoulder and her hand caressing my leg. We talked about all sorts of rubbish, who was seeing who in school, what music we loved and hated, where our families were from, life death, politics. All the time we were relaxed and comfortable, as if we have been close for years.

Once at Leicester square we stopped at Café Nero for a coffee and a muffin, then across the square for some Hagen Daas ice cream. We wrapped our arms around each other and fed each other in turn. I had rum and raisin, Sasha had chocolate and fudge. It was amazing, especially as I hate fudge so much; even shit food tastes amazing around Sasha!

We watched the film that I have seen a million and 2 times and she laughed all the way through it and I laughed with her. Every time she laughed I had to look over at her and see the effect it had upon her face, laughs had a way of lighting her up. I enjoyed the film just as much as I did the first time I saw it.

After the film we walked through the streets of London, not knowing where we were going, laughing stopping to kiss and popping into the occasional shop to look around. We eventually ended up in Bond St (which on a map seems like we walked quite some distance from Leicester Square!).

We took our tube to Victoria and cuddled up on our train back to Brighton. When we got back to Worthing I walked her home and we kissed for nearly an hour outside her house, after which I pretty much skipped all the way home and got in at about half past twelve. I am pretty sure I am in love with her, or at least falling fast. I have spent the whole day with her, and still want to be with her. I do actually miss her; I have a funny little ache in my stomach when I think of her. Surely that's what love is? Or maybe I'm just going a little bit soft?

Why can all days be like this!!

**Monday, February 13th**

After the best Sunday in history (or any day for that matter!), it was obviously going to be the blandest and most boring day today, and it didn't let me down. Sasha was out at her nans today, Martin was heading to a campsite in northern France somewhere with his dad and I was stuck in doors revising and yearning for someone to talk to or just something to do to break the monotony.

I have been thinking about this love thing and I am interested in hearing what other people think on this subject, so I have started my own little project (may even lead me to writing a book on the subject one day I suppose). I thought that a good place to start would be with my parents. They do seem to get on ok, but I wouldn't exactly say that they were in love, but maybe I'm wrong. I am interested to know whether it has always been this way, or were things different when they were younger?

I asked both my parents the same question: "What is love?"

My mum was quite blunt about this and seems to feel that love doesn't really exist. "It's something that young people do." She said. I then asked her if she was in love with dad, she replied. "Look Matt, either buggar off or lend a hand!" I will ask her again when she is not stressed out by the huge pile of dirty dishes and endless loads of laundry she was putting in and out of the washing machine.

My dad gave me a much more interesting answer, can't quote him exactly but it was something like this: "I love you, your brother and your mum. I suppose it's about really caring for someone so much that you would do anything for them, even die for them. I was lucky to have great parents too, but your mum wasn't. Her dad was always gambling away the shopping money and she never had anything growing up. Her old man was never at home, and on the rare occasion that he was he was usually so drunk and angry that no one dare go near him. I really believe that he would have sold your mother for a couple of beers and a bit of money for the horses. So just being related is no guarantee of love! So I suppose what I am saying that love is about taking responsibility for someone you care about and doing what you can to make sure that they are happy".

Wise words from the ol' man.

I don't think I am in love just yet. I really like Sasha, but if it was life or death between the 2 of us, it's a no brainer. I'd even put the bullet in her myself!

## Tuesday, February 14th

I spoke to Sasha today and we are meeting up tomorrow, 'at her house!' because her 'parents are away!!' Holy shit, are we going to have sex?

I do have a bit of a dilemma going on in my head about this situation. I'm not 100% sure that I am ready to actually have sex with Sasha at the moment. Don't get me wrong, I fancy the pants off her, how couldn't I, she really is damn hot. But I really don't want to ruin things by going too fast. I am worried that if we had sex things may get a little weird between us, especially if I am utter rubbish at this sex thing (which I fully expect to be by the way!) I think I like her and respect her far too much to take such a massive step like this sex thing too soon. I am pretty sure that this does not mean I am gay however.

Truth be told, I am nervous about this 'meet up'. Everything I have done today, pick up a pen, wash some dishes, walk to the shops to buy some bread, I have done to the faint tingle of butterflies in my slightly flabby stomach. The fact is, we will probably just end up watching a film and chatting and not having sex at all. After all we have only been a couple for 6 days. I did however decided to buy a packet of condoms at the shops today, just in case.

Some people seem to think that buying condoms is a difficult thing to do; I don't get this at all. This was my first time buying condoms and I have heard that some people get incredibly nervous when they approach the counter. I simply walked in, grabbed a pack (durex gossamer by the way) and proudly handed them to the young girl behind the counter and paid with a bit of a smirk on my face. It was like I was effectively saying to the shop assistant, "Hello, I am going to have 3 shags!" What's wrong with that? ………nothing, that's what. If anything I felt incredible proud!

I managed 40 press ups and 50 sit ups this evening. I even managed a 10 min jog around the local park. I figured that if we are going to have sex, then she will have to see me naked, which is a little scary in itself. It is therefore only fair that I make a little bit of an effort to not look so much like Jabba the Hut.

I 'borrowed' my dad's lap top and did a little bit of searching to pick up a few tips. The World Wide Web is indeed a very dirty place!! I have to admit to getting a little side tracked from my initial search, but think I have deleted everything that I looked at. It is my dad's work computer and he would go mental if he knew that I had looked at such sites as 'www.giant-teen-tits.com'!

## Wednesday, February 15th

Pretty sure that when all is said and done, and when I cash out from this life. Today will be the best day of my life!

I carefully packed all of my 3 durex gossamer condoms into my mini jeans pocket, checked my breath and left for Sasha's. I arrived at Sasha's at around 12:30pm and she answered the door in her dressing gown. Her gown was a bit too open at the top allowing easy boob viewing access, which was very nice. They are certainly nice boobs, not quite the same as those I witnessed on 'www.giant-teen-tits.com', but very nice. From the magazines and page 3's I have 'studied' over the years, I would guess at a bra size of 34 C. I can honestly say that I have never really taken a great deal of notice in them before and just how great they are. Perhaps I really do need my eyes testing after all.
She lunged at me on the doorstep and gave me a really passionate kiss, I had an instant erection. Because of this I did not enjoy the kiss as much as I should have. I was far too busy trying to pull my groin away while maintaining my effective mouth lock. I did not think she would appreciate being stabbed in the stomach by my rouge erect penis.

She led me by the hand into the lounge, poured me a glass of wine and put on some music....The Smiths! As we established earlier dear diary, I love The Smiths. Fair play..... Probably not the most romantic choice of music in the world, but this chick certainly has class! 'I was happy in the haze of a drunken hour….' I had only had a sip of wine, but I was certainly in a haze. I am not a big drinker either, so knew I would really have to watch myself.

We sat on the sofa and my stomach was turning over and over with a dangerous concoction of wine, excitement and nerves. She took my wine from me, put it on the table and kissed me while pushing me back.

The sofa was made from a very soft black leather with an unearthly cold feel to it. There were buttons on it!!?? That's weird, why put buttons on a sofa. I deliberately focused on these things as I was trying to calm myself down. I was getting worried that either my stomach would explode or the excess blood in my groinal region would leave my brain in deficit and lead me to pass out. To make matters even worse I developed a sudden need to fart. Not just a little one, but a huge, 'oh my god my eyes are stinging' one that could not only end this relationship in one brown gust, but one which could also endanger both our lives.

She ran her fingers through my hair and caressed the back of my neck. I just lay there trying to decide whether I should have my eyes open or closed? One of life's great mysteries I suppose, I chose closed in the end – after all, I had a massive fart to concentrate on suppressing. Questions rifled through my head as my panic continued:

"Am I doing this right?"
"Is she enjoying this too?"
"Oh my god is my breath still ok?"
"What is the capital of Ecuador?" - (This question was on a quiz show I watched last night and I missed the answer when my mum called me for dinner).
"Why is the sky blue?"

I got a little braver and put my hands around her back and started to caress her hair. We must have been kissing for about 5 minutes and my lips were getting a little numb. I guessed that hers must have been too as she started to just use her tongue. She used it to caress my tongue first, then my lips, then chin and then she was on my neck. It struck me at this point that we had not even actually said hello to each other.

Having your neck kissed simply has to be why God put us on the Earth; I wanted to die there and then as surely life would never be that good again!

While she worked her magic around my neck she grabbed my right hand and guided it into her dressing gown and onto her breast, her naked perfect breast. Things were getting pretty serious now!

Her skin was $1000^{\circ}C$. I squeezed her gently, not really knowing what I was expected to do. Her skin was soft and the texture made my head spin. I brushed my finger against her nipple and she let out a soft moan, starred intensely into my eyes, smiled and then playfully bit my bottom lip.

I had a horrible feeling that if she were to suddenly decide touch 'downstairs' I would have been unable to control myself! I had to quickly try and think of stuff to help me keep it together as I was starting to feel myself spiraling out of control with the intensity of this situation.

"My Nan's facial hair."
"Runny dog shit."
"Sasha's naked perfect breast! Sasha's naked perfect breast!" – No, no, no, try harder!
"Faggots and peas." – I hate Faggots and detest peas!
"Nan's moustache, Nan's beard."
"A shaking shitting dog."
"Sasha's naked perfect breast! Sasha's naked perfect breast!" – It was clearly no use!

Then she touched 'downstairs'! I just about managed to keep it together. This obviously felt very nice, but I just felt so nervous and venerable that I don't think I really enjoyed it as much as I should have. I did wonder why, that during the most intimate and exciting moment of my life to date, I was unable to just go with it and enjoy it. Instead I felt myself just laying back against the insanely 'cold buttoned black leather sofa', holding in a deadly fart as tense as an iron bar imagining my hairy Nan walking a shaking shitting dog with diarrhea!

"Let's go upstairs" She whispered in my ear.

I managed a nod, popped into the bathroom, farted for what felt like 5 minutes, checked my tackle and skipped off to have sex for the first time in my life.

Dear diary, some things I am afraid I just won't share. The only thing I will say is that it was amazing, not as short as I was worried about and that it happened 3 times! I knew I should have bought the bigger pack from the chemist!

We spent the rest of the afternoon in her bed watching rubbish telly, laughing and cuddling.

But the best part of the whole day for me was when Sasha said:

"That was my first time"

Wow! I had assumed that as she is so hot, she must have had sex before, at least once. She was far more confident than me as well and really did seem to know what she was doing.

She also told me that she loved me, I told her I loved her too (I am pretty sure I was telling the truth as well). I am now officially in a proper adult relationship and I am officially a man.

Quito, btw.

## Thursday, February 16<sup>th</sup>

Sasha has gone up North (Liverpool way I think) today with her family to visit an Aunt that isn't very well, and I am at a loose end. Luckily Martin was in the same situation so I spent the morning revising and then popped into Brighton with him. I told him about yesterday, although not in any degree of detail no matter how much he prodded!

We sat in Costa coffee and had a couple of lattes and a muffin each and then went bowling. As I mentioned before I am awful at bowling and always lose, it's a bloody irritating game that really does look a hell of a lot easier than it actually is. As usual my lane was surrounded on either side by fucking professionals who seemed to get a strike with every bowl. I managed 1 all afternoon. I watched them for a little while, all of them seemed to have a magical ability to make the ball swerve all over the shop before angling into the side of the first pin and then smashing them down in a kind of domino effect, it really is quite impressive. However, let's not forget that it is a stupid game, which really pisses me off, I have no idea why I agreed to play.

Needless to say Martin hammered me and spent the rest of the day gloating and doing impressions of my pathetic bowling technique. He described it as "Rather like an 80-year-old lady with a hunchback doing a shit while falling forwards off the toilet." Pretty accurate really.

We stopped at HMV and looked through the 100's of exciting games that neither of us could afford, before catching the bus back home. I did make a purchase however, 'Hatful of Hollow' by The Smith's, the theme tune to the best day of my life! Quite ironic that it contains the song, 'Heaven knows I'm miserable now'!

I spoke to Sasha in the evening, she has only been away for a few hours in reality but it's hard to describe just how much I miss her. It feels like when you are watching a really exciting film that is getting near the end and your dad walks in turns over and simply says, "News!" Sasha is due back on Saturday evening and we have made plans to go bowling on Sunday. God I hate bowling.

Has having sex made the relationship weird? Nope! It's made me want to be with her all the time (and obviously have sex, all the time too). I think I have found a new hobby, one which I want to become very good at. I am really looking forward to the practice.

I spent the evening doing a bit of revision while listening to my new CD. Teachers who say, "You can't possibly revise while listening to music." Are full of crap, I did loads this evening and it pretty much all sunk in.

Why don't they make sex an Olympic sport? Then I would have to practice extra hard. Maybe even 7 hours a day. On second thoughts, that may prove to make things a little bit sore.

**Friday, February 17th**

Today has been a nightmare!

All was going well in the morning. We had a nice full breakfast as Dad had the day off work and he decided to knock up one of his specials. I did a bit of revision, had a bit of a kick around in the garden with Ollie and then things went very wrong.

"Matt get your ass in here!" Shouted my dad. It wasn't a friendly 'get your ass in here!' but a nasty, aggressive and hateful 'get your ass in here!' There was no two ways about it, I was in deep shit about something.

I sheepishly wandered into the house to see what the hell I had done. My brain was racing all over the place……Just what had I done? Ah, I remembered……

"What the hell is this!?" My dad pointed to his laptop.

"Anal treasures!! Have you been looking at porn on my work laptop!?"

I immediately turned tomato red and squeaked "Yes, sorry". I suppose I could have lied, I could have denied it, but I think that would only have prolonged the misery and embarrassment. I thought that it was a much better idea to face this one like a man. An Anal treasures, porn loving man.

"It's not bad enough you have been looking at porn, but to do it on my work laptop! What the hell were you thinking? And anal porn what the hell is the matter with you?"

"I'm sorry ok, what can I say" I was dying. I don't think I have ever been as embarrassed. I fully wanted a hole to open up and swallow me. Then I wanted a black hole to open up and swallow that previous hole, reduce me and all the matter that I was made of into the size of an atom and spew me into an entirely new universe, infinitely far away from my fathers disgusted stare.

But it didn't. So I just stood there, bright red with shame.

"I am ashamed of you, its lucky that I spotted it as well. Imagine if bloody anal treasures popped up during a meeting! I would lose my job Matt! You really are a fucking idiot at times!"

This bollocking went on for quite some time. It took the predictable format of me saying I was 'sorry' and him calling me either an 'idiot' or a 'fucking idiot'. It finished with him sending me to my room and banning me for life from his laptop. Fair enough I suppose.

When my mum came back from work she joined in with the humiliation process.

"What bothers me most Matt is not that you were looking at porn, I can sort of understand that. But that you were probably wanking away in our living room! What if one of our neighbors saw you? How would you live that down? How would any of us live that down?"

Again I could only really manage a "Sorry".

As I changed for bed I noticed that my penis was covered in tiny red spots, I obviously now think I have either syphilis, gonorrhea, herpes, HIV or all of them and some others diseases I have not heard of yet. I imagine that I will probably be dead within a week. At least the embarrassment would go away then.

Now it's started to itch as well.

I don't think this is quite what Lou Reed had in mind when he wrote the song 'perfect day'.


### Saturday, February 18th

I spent the day alone, in shame in my bedroom. I was too embarrassed to face my parents. God knows what they must think of me.

I am officially an 'anal loving, spotted cocked loser' it's a good job Sasha is still away. I didn't speak to her yesterday, it just didn't feel appropriate!

Sasha gets back from the North today. Unfortunately she is not going to get back until around 8:30 in the evening and will probably be tired, so I will catch up with her tomorrow. Luckily it's just bowling and not sex, I definitely will not be able to have sex while I have an acute dose of 'cock pox'!

These little red spots on my manhood are really worrying me, they itch and look like they are getting worse. If they don't look any better tomorrow I suppose I had better go and see the Doctor. I don't fancy having to do that, the woman in the surgery reception is a right nosey old shit bag. She pretty much thinks she is the Doctor at the surgery and wants to know everything, I imagine that the conversation would probably play out as follows:

Me - Can I have an appointment to see the Doctor please?
Nosey Old Shit Bag - Why what's wrong with you?
Me – Oh, it's a problem I have downstairs.
Nosey Old Shit Bag – What exactly is the problem?
Me – Something to do with my 'man area'.
Nosey Old Shit Bag – Can you describe the problem to me please sir.
Me – I would rather do that with a Doctor if it's all the same with you.
Nosey Old Shit Bag – I am afraid all the Doctors are very busy and only seeing genuine emergencies. Is this a genuine emergency?
Me – Yes, I appear to have a rather nasty disease of the cock! It's covered in red spots, itches like a bastard and it threatening to fall off at any moment!

Now book me a fucking appointment you sad, old, smelly cacky fingered old witch and stop asking me anymore questions! Else I will unleash it from my trousers and belt you across the head with it!!

Well, maybe not the last bit…..

I checked my emails this evening. You know you have been looking at websites that you shouldn't have when you receive emails entitled: '8 hours of big tits! Free!' Made me chuckle. 8 hours of big tits is probably a bit too long. In my limited experience, 20 minutes would probably be plenty!

### Sunday, February 19th

I love bowling! I am obviously still rubbish at it (even Sasha beat me!) but going bowling with Sasha has changed my opinion. I think what swung it for me was the fact that I got to stare at Sasha's perfectly formed buttocks for a good 30 seconds whenever it was her turn to bowl. Weird really, she is my girlfriend after all; surely I should just be able to ask to look at it whenever I want to, maybe even naked! I love bowling and I love leggings even more.

After we had finished bowling, Sasha and I took a walk along the sea front. It was absolutely freezing. The wind drove ice cold rain into our faces and the sea was mercilessly smashing into the pebbles making an almighty noise. But this just added to the romance of it for me. We huddled together, stumbling against the weather and giggling as we went. We stopped and sat for a couple of minutes on a bench to cuddle and kiss before heading off home to thaw out and dry off.

On another positive note, the little red spots on my penis seem to have gone!! Hooray, I am sexually transmitted disease, pox and itch free and ready for action!

## Monday, February 20th

Back to school today, not such a bad thing really. At least I get to see Sasha every day. Ordinarily I would have been pretty gutted to have been going back.

Sasha and I have become one of those pathetic couples around the school playground that I have always hated. We hold hands all the time, kiss each other and giggle constantly. I just wish that I was in more of her lessons. A little sad I know, but I have honestly never been happier.

I walked Sasha home after school and kissed on her door step for nearly half an hour. Unfortunately her mum was in and sex was not on the menu.

"No one is in tomorrow lunch time" Sasha whispered in my ear, and then bit it. I know that she did it in a kind of 'playful, but sexy' way, but it bloody hurt. The weird thing is that I really liked it, perhaps I'm one of those S&M type fellas who's into whips, chains and candle wax on nipples.

I walked home with a huge erection (by huge I obviously mean for me, and for me I mean average size for the UK. I've Googled it!) and a throbbing ear lobe.

The whole 'internet porn scandal' seems to have blown over which is great. My parents have stopped looking at me as if I have just taken a dump on the kitchen table. Time is a great healer.

I spent the majority of my evening shut up in my room revising. I figured that staying out of everyone's way and getting my head down was the best way to smooth over things with the olds.

## Tuesday, February 21st

I literally leaped out of bed this morning. As soon as my antiquated Bart Simpson clock struck its first note I was wide awake and thinking just one thing. Lunchtime! I rushed downstairs, grabbed a piece of toast from Ollie's plate and shot out the door to meet Martin. We stopped off to pick up Sasha on the way to. Sasha and I were both beaming at each other all the way to school, so much so that Martin felt compelled to asked, "What the hell are you two up to?"

"Nothing." We both said in unison.

The fact was that neither of us could wait until lunch time. My lessons today were a complete write off; my head was away with the fairies. When the lunch bell rang I pretty much sprinted out of the Chemistry lab and headed to meet Sasha at the school gates. We kissed briefly and jogged off hand in hand to her house. When we arrived there we slammed the door behind us and started tearing each other's clothes off while stumbling towards the stairs. Sasha paused. "Mum!" She shouted. We waited for what seemed a lifetime………

No answer….. Nice!

By the time we were half way up the stairs we were both fully naked and ready for action, Sasha grabbed me and started to pull me in. I froze in fear, I had no condoms! In my child like excitement I had completely forgotten about buying some, how could I have been so stupid? I was just about to announce this bombshell when Sasha whispered, "it's ok, I'm on the pill".

The rest dear diary is once again between me, Sasha, a flight of stairs, a neighbor's cat and a rather unfortunate teddy bear. The only thing I will say is that I have noticed that sex definitely has a smell, a strange smell. Does all sex smell the same? Or is it different for different couples? I will have to Google it (obviously not on Dad's work computer). We were quite brief in our 'lovemaking' (well, we are both new to this activity) and just managed to get back to school for afternoon registration.

If I was unproductive in school in the morning, then the afternoon more than made up for it! I don't remember ever working so hard, both my French and English teachers commented on this fact. Lunchtime sex sessions should therefore be made compulsory in all secondary schools.

On a slightly sour note on what was an otherwise perfect day I found out through one of Sasha's friend that Todd has had a massive crush on her for ages and has caught wind of the fact that we are together and is not happy. This is bound to lead to some grief; the guy really is an incredible fuckwit.

By the way, the cat was not involved…..just present.

## Wednesday, February 22$^{nd}$

Things have really kicked off today. Martin is in hospital with 2 broken ribs and a fractured jaw.

You guessed it dear diary; Todd was indeed behind this one. Martin had not done a lot wrong in all honesty, he is no fighter and always tends to avoid trouble generally. In fact I can't think of a time that he has ever had an argument with anyone, let alone a fight.

I think that Todd clearly has some mental health issues at the moment. Rumor has it that he is taking all sorts of drugs and that he may even be dabbling with heroin now, it may sound unlikely for a 16 to have reached this level, but he really does have a very distant look in his eyes. They say that some soldiers develop a thousand yard stare after being involved in combat, Todd has certainly not been to war recently, but he definitely does have a thousand yard stare. Unfortunately (or fortunately depending on how you look at it) I was not actually there when the incident occurred, but I did manage to get the full story from a group of girls in my year.

Martin was apparently walking down the science corridor on his way to English and Todd kicked his trailing leg behind the other one, and he stumbled forward dropping the books and files he was carrying. Martin turned around and said:

"You fucking prick!"

This was quite unlike a typical Martin reply, I would have expected a more sarcastic response, but this was all the invitation that Todd needed and exactly the response he wanted. Todd lunged at Martin and swung a massive haymaker at him. The punch made contact, big contact. He had managed to knock Martin out cold with one blow to the jaw. If that wasn't enough, Todd then set about kicking and stamping on Martin, as he lay unconscious in the corridor. Todd's friend Ryan put in a final sickening boot to the head before the pair of them ran off.

Martin suffered a concussion, 2 broken ribs and a small fracture to the side of his jaw. His body was literally covered in bruises and was taken to hospital where he is probably going to remain for a day or two for observations.

The police were at the school in a shot. They arrested Todd and bundled him into the back of their car. They took statements from a number of witnesses before driving off with a smiling and fully defiant Todd waving from the back of the police car with hands rightly in cuffs. I really hope that police brutality is alive and well in West Sussex, as if anyone needs a kicking it is this guy.

Rumor around the school is that Todd is going to be permanently excluded for this day's work, about time if you ask me! I still have no idea why he has an issue with the 2 of us; he probably doesn't even know himself though. I have been waiting for some kind of confrontation with Todd because of the Sasha situation, and I hope this has not been the reason for Martin being beaten up.

I went to see Martin at hospital with my parents after school today and he was in surprisingly good spirits, despite not being able to speak very well he still said: "As long as it gets him expelled, it was worth the beating!"
Martin said that he is due out of hospital on Saturday. Apparently the doctors were reluctant to let him go home until the swelling on his head had started to reduce in size. The police had visited Martin earlier

in the day and taken a statement about the incident. Martin has decided to press charges against Todd. Nice, I hope they lock him up and throw away the key, or better still: beat him mercilessly about the face and chest with a broken bottle, cut his cock off, lock him up and throw away the key.

## Thursday, February 23rd

Today was another mad one, it really does seem as if they all are at the moment.

School was quite hectic today. I think that every single member of the school community has now asked me how Martin is getting on. This includes: Students, teachers, teaching assistants, dinner ladies and premises staff. I was half expecting the dead frozen mice in the Science labs to awake from their wintery graves and bloody well ask me too. The hassle was so intense that I nearly decided to make a sign and put it around my neck saying 'Martin is in a bit of pain, but will be out of hospital on Saturday and he is doing well! Now fuck off!' Well, maybe not the 'fuck off!' bit, but it really was getting a bit much. I saw Todd on his way in to the heads office and waved at him, smiled sweetly and mouthed out "Bye bye". Probably not the wisest thing I have ever done. Todd tried to run at me but was caught by the arm by the Deputy Head so decided to shout at me instead: "You're a fucking dead man, watch. When I see you around or your slag of a misses I will fuck you and her up!"

"I will look forward to it." Was all I could offer as a reply, but I did blow him a very sweet kiss.
"Get to your lesson!!" shouted the deputy head.

Todd was indeed permanently expelled today (no surprise there) and his sidekick Ryan has been externally excluded for 5 days for violent conduct.

Martin was delighted with the news! Sasha and I visited him at hospital after school and took him some grapes (Sasha's idea, not mine). He was feeling a lot better, but his ribs were very tender and he had to stay still all the time, only being able to fall asleep on his side with his right arm over his head to take the pressure off of his ribs. We all sat on his bed and watched EastEnders and some of the champion's league game between Liverpool and Roma, I am not a huge football fan (if pushed I suppose I would have to say I am a Brighton fan – support your local team and all that) but I have a particular hate for Liverpool (Todd is a Liverpool fan and often wears a Liverpool shirt. I especially hate them now after Sasha revealed that her parents are all Everton fans too).

Martin was not particularly pleased when Roma scored the first goal (Martin always supports the British clubs in these competitions) and Sasha and I jumping up and down in celebration, jolting poor Martin all over the shop in the process couldn't have helped. The swellings on Martin's head have gone down a lot and all being well he should be going home tomorrow morning after the Doctor checks him over.

**Friday, February 24th**

I got jumped in the playground today. Even though Todd has been expelled, he still unfortunately seems to have a big influence on all of the major idiots of the school.

I was walking across the playground to the Math's block and was suddenly jumped by 4 of Todd's henchmen. I got away pretty much unscathed, but it did shake me up a bit. I felt someone jump on my back then someone kicked me in the back of the legs pretty hard, at which point I went down. All 4 of them gathered around and started kicking me while I was on the floor until the Head of Math's shouted out of the window at them, at which point they legged it in various directions.

I have no idea who they were, although I am pretty sure they were year 9 students, but it's a big school and it's unlikely that I will learn the identity of all of them. One of them however had ginger hair and a green Nike hoodie – I think he is probably the only one I would recognize again, I will certainly be keeping my eyes peeled for that little ginger glass of toss!
As they stopped kicking the piss out of me and ran, one of them shouted "That's from Todd you fucking prick, he is gonna fuck you up!" Charming use of the English language I thought.

As for my injuries, none really, I have actually gotten off pretty lightly all things considered. A grazed hand

and a bleeding elbow (with matching ripped shirt – which will probably result in worse injuries from my Mother when I get home).

Sasha and I are off to Brighton tomorrow for a bit of shopping and some chips by the sea, nice. Oh, and a new shirt. Sasha and I talked about the whole 'jumping' situation on the way home. She has made me promise to her that I won't go and do something silly. Not too sure that it is one that I will be able to keep if I find myself face to face with that chavy ginger anus.

They have decided to keep Martin in for one further night as his ribs have really been playing up and they have decided to do another x-ray to make sure there is nothing 'floating' about. Sounds grim. I do hope that is not something that Sasha and I caused during our dramatic goal celebration.

## Saturday, February 25$^{th}$

Martin came home this morning and Sasha and I decided to pop around and see him before we went off to Brighton. He was laid out on the sofa and was watching Red Dwarf. The Doctors were happy that his swelling had gone down enough and that his ribs weren't too badly cracked and he would be good enough to move about as normal within 2 weeks. Sasha and I had a cup of tea watched an episode of Red Dwarf and then headed off to get our bus.

Poor ol' Martin still has to lay with his right arm around the top of his head. I have never broken a rib and never want to, it sounds awful, it doesn't seem like you can do anything to help with the pain, you just have to wait until it heals. Martin does seem quite happy with his prescription of painkillers though, he says they seem to make things a lot more 'colourful'.

Brighton was pleasant; we sat in a quiet coffee shop at the sea front for about 3 hours just chatting. We only actually bought 2 drinks each in this time and I am sure the owner was giving us evil looks, not that it was busy.

Sasha has invited me around to hers tomorrow day time....parents away, score! She has also invited me for dinner in the evening when they get back, I have said yes, but I am very nervous about meeting them, I mean what the hell am I supposed to say when I shake her dad's hand?

"Hi, I'm Matt! I am banging your daughter!"

### Sunday, February 26th

After what seemed like 5 hours of bathroom preparation I went to Sasha's and spent the day having sex and cuddling. I think we are really getting good now, it is not so nervy and we are both a lot more relaxed.

I experienced my first oral sex today. Wow, now that is what I'm talking about! I performed and was performed upon. Performing was amazing, but the latter nearly made me pass out.

After my amazing morning at Sasha's I popped in on Martin to see how he was getting on. Martin found out yesterday that the police were not going to be following up with the charges that he had pressed against Todd. He is pretty gutted about it and I am staggered by the complete lack of justice in this silly country. Apparently no one else would back up Martin's story, so there was just not enough evidence to proceed. Surely, a broken jaw and ribs is evidence enough? I guess that the fear of being beaten up by that tosser must have got to all of the witnesses. Martin and I vegged out and watched Deep Blue Sea. A rather enjoyable shark thriller, in a nutshell it is: Clever sharks eating the shit out of crap actors.

If ever Sasha and I split up and I enter a relationship with someone else, here is a list of things that I will not do when I meet 'their' parents for the first time:

- Arrive late for dinner (my mum insisted that I washed the dishes before I left for Sasha's – cheers Mum!)
- Appear on the front door (opened by both Sasha's Mum and Dad by the way), panting and with my flies fully undone. To top this off, Sasha's mum's introductory comment was, "You must be Matt, do you realize your flies are undone?"

- Step on the cats' tail. Twice.
- Break a dinner plate by dropping a knife onto it
- Say 'shit!' after dropping my knife onto my plate
- Cut myself on a piece of broken plate, created by my dropping a knife on it while saying 'shit!'
- Say 'bollocks!' after cutting myself on a piece of broken plate created by my dropping a knife on it while saying 'shit!'
- Cough with a mouthful of food, firing a bolas of spaghetti across the table.

Sasha obviously thought all of this was hysterical and spent the majority of my entertaining visit laughing to the point of tears, but I have never been so embarrassed. I think it's probably the last time I will ever be invited over for dinner! It will be a lot cheaper for them to keep me away, what with all the crockery they will have to replace and the very expensive vet's bills.

### Monday, February 27th

School was very good today; I had a science test and not only answered all the questions, but I would even go as far to sat that I think I have actually done pretty well too. So much so that I didn't quite have enough time to finish as well as I would like. At has to be a good sign. I am quite a quick writer (quick and very untidy actually) and usually finish exams with enough time for a good 30 minute snooze.

Sasha and I stopped at Lickin' Chicken on the way home. I the 3 piece and chips and her, the veggie burger. The way my stomach is cart wheeling at the moment, I feel the veggie burger was the winning choice! The amount of pure fat I have ingested is very grim indeed. I still feel kind of nauseous now, in fact….

…Yep, just vomited – lovely, stomach is still turning over quite a bit too. This is not going to look pretty on the way out the 'other end'. The shop should be renamed "Shittin' Chicken" I think. It's the last time I go there!

**Tuesday, February 28th**

I have spent most of today either in bed or on the toilet with great thanks to the chefs at "Shittin' Chicken". Needless to say I didn't go into school today. I am not often ill so Mum and Dad didn't give me too much grief about missing a day of school, but my Dad did ring at lunchtime to ensure I was genuine and not having a Ferris Bueller episode. I have been firing out of both ends at high velocity all day! It is quite a skill to maintain a steady stream out of you bum while stretching to throw up in the sink, but I seem to have mastered that one. The only major pain in the ass (pardon the expression), is having to scoop up the chunks from the sink and fling them into the toilet on top of the patiently awaiting liquidy crap. Not nice at all.

Sasha rang me this evening and told me about her day. Todd had been at the school gates at the end of the day and slapped her face (she did slap him first though which is good). Apparently he stood in front of her as she tried to leave the school and asked her "why are you wasting your time with that tosser when you can have a real man? Have you fucked him? I bet he has a tiny cock?" This was the point that she slapped him (defending my honor! That's my girl!). Then, being the decent human being he undoubtable is, he slapped her back and called her a slag. He really has got it coming to him if I run into him on his own, nutter or not I will punch him out – even if it does mean I take a kicking.

Must dash, my bowels are calling. Actually, not so much calling, more shouting!

# **March**

## **Wednesday, March 1ˢᵗ**

Science result back today, A*, 92% - My parents now love me again. I am officially the new Stephen Hawkings! It really is the first time I have ever done so well in a test. This revision lark does actually seem to be paying off.

I caught up with that little ginger tosser today. I saw him walking down the corridor in the humanities block. The corridor was pretty quiet so I figured I would get away with a stealthy attack. I jogged up behind him and shouted, "Ginger!" Ok, probably not the most imaginative insult, but it was certainly loud enough and full of venom.

He spun around and I punched him as hard as I could just above his left eye. His skin split and blood ran out immediately and he dropped to his knees and clutched his face and with that I was off. That is what I call justice, an eye for an eye and all that. I only wish I could remember what all the others looked like too, but the word should quickly get around that jumping me is not a wise move.

Sasha went mad with me at the end of the day. I was a little bit surprised by just how mad though. I knew I was in trouble when I saw her standing waiting for me at the school gates. He arms were folded and she looked thoroughly pissed off.

"Why the fuck have you gone and done that, you really are an idiot!" Wow, this was the first time I have ever heard her swear like that. The occasional shit, damn and words like that. But never a fuck.

"Now you have given Todd even more reason to hate you, not that he need any! What am I supposed to do when he comes into school and stabs you?" Sasha really was talking loud and I was a little bit embarrassed about the situation. I tried explaining that I thought this was a clear warning and that it would be the end of the issue, but she fully disagreed with that. To be fair, I didn't really believe it either.

"This won't be the end of it; the guy is a fucking nutter. He will come here and he is just stupid enough to bring something with him! A knife, a bat or maybe even worse. You really have to keep a very low profile around here over the next few weeks and make sure you avoid Todd at all costs. He will come for you, I fucking guarantee it."

As she finished saying this she turned and stormed off home leaving me rushing behind her trying desperately to keep up. We didn't say a word all the way home, and even then, when we reached the gate to her house all I could actually manage was "Sorry." I pecked her on the cheek and turned for home.

On reflection, my actions were probably not the most sensible, but I do think Sasha has over reacted a little here. As big an idiot as Todd is, he isn't the knife wielding, gun toting maniac she thinks he is. He is just a bit of a twat who thinks he is a little bit of a gangster and whose parents never really loved him enough.

**Thursday, March 2nd**

Martin came back to school this morning. He is still a little uncomfortable, but his dad dropped him in and gave him money to get a taxi home at the end of the day. He will be fine; it will just take a little bit of time for him to adjust.

I walked into school with Sasha and she apologised for losing her temper with me. She said, "Its only because I love you and worry about you, I would hate something to happen to you. Things between us just been so perfect Matt and I don't want that to change." I apologised for my actions and we left it at that.

I have been working very hard recently and the Science result has really spurred me on a lot. I have a French test next week and have been putting in the hours to ensure that I get a similar result to the Science one. It's nice to have happy parents and I would like to keep them that way! And besides, the whole computer porn issue seems to be ancient history now.

On the way home after school, Sasha and I talked about the possibility of going camping in the Easter holidays. I am not too sure how my parents would react, I guess not well. It might be a better idea to get a group of us together and go camping. That way I can easily dupe my parents into thinking I will be going with Martin and not sauntering off for a filthy weekend with my beautiful girlfriend. The idea of some pure unadulterated sexy time together does sound amazing though. So I'm in!

## Friday, March 3rd

After a very ordinary and non-eventful day at school came the most full on and frightening end to the school day I have ever had.

As the end of school bell rang out I left my Math's classroom and started to head over towards the school gates where I usually meet Sasha to walk home. As I got closer I couldn't see her, not unusual I thought – perhaps she was stopping back after school to finish some work. At times like that I often reflected on the horrible fact that I must be the only kid in year 11 without a mobile phone (cheers mum and dad). As I continued towards the gates I could however see a large group of lads hanging around. A few of them appeared to be on bikes, all of them seemed to be wearing hoodies. I slowed right down and then stopped as a cold wave crashed over my body and a scream developed in the back of my mouth.

Todd was there, this was 'his' little shitty gang and I didn't doubt for a second that they were waiting for me. I quickly turned and started walking back towards the Math's block. As soon as I did I heard one of his goons shout out, "There he is!"

I looked briefly over my left shoulder and saw the group coming into the school grounds. There were 4 or 5 of them on bikes who were already gaining on me. I broke out into a pretty fast sprint as I didn't fancy my chances against this many idiots. They gained on me pretty fast and when I was about 5 meters from the Math's block doors I felt hands grab my back and shoulders as one of them lunged at me from his bike. He grabbed hold hard and fell forwards from his bike taking me down to my knees. I stepped up and turned at the same time breaking his now weakened hold on me. I placed a well-aimed kick straight in his chest and he fell and rolled over, moaning in pain. 2 more on bikes jumped off and started to run at me. I span again and quickly leapt inside the Math's block slamming the floor bolt into place. The 2 lads (who I did not recognize) barged into the door with full force and the top of the door buckled in about a foot. As soon as they recoiled and got ready to try again, I slammed the top bolt in place as well. Their second barge was well repelled by the thankfully heavy math's door and I knew I was safe, for a while at least.

I stood for a moment, breathing heavily trying to compose myself and thinking all the time about how I was going to get out of this situation.

I looked out of the Math's block doors. The 2 lads were still there, hammering with fists and kicking away trying to get in. The lad I had kicked was back on his feet and walking towards the doors to rejoin the assault. Another lad on a bike, who must have been at least 20 got off and joined in with door banging, while a little way back the rest of Todd's group, with Todd himself in the middle were walking over to join them.

The 20 year old had a green Adidas hoody on and although closely shaven, it was easy to make out some distinct ginger hair. He must have been that ginger tossers brother. The banging stopped and he confirmed my thoughts and said:

"You hit my brother you fuck, when we get you man, we are going to fucking tear you up!"

I am pretty sure he meant that! He was at least 6 foot tall and looked full of both muscle and menace. Not someone I would fancy my chances against, that's for sure. Then he turned and said "Todd, hurry up with that bat! You pricks go and find another way in!"

Unfortunately for me I knew damn well that there were another 3 ways into the building and there was no way I was going to be able to stop them getting in. Todd arrived with his bat and started swinging at the door. The door was obviously very well made and must have contained reinforced glass as the first hit was pretty fierce but simply bounced off with absolutely no effect. I wasn't going to hang around to find out just how good the door was though and quickly ran off, turned the corner and head up the stairs. I got about three quarters of the way up when I heard an almighty smash. They were in.

The Math's block only has a ground floor and first floor. When I got to the top of the stairs I turned left and headed down the corridor. Even though the bell for the end of the day had just gone the top floor of Math's was deserted. There must have been a staff meeting on. I tried the handle on the first classroom I came to, it was locked. Tried the next on my right, again locked. I worked my way rapidly down the corridor trying all the doors as I went getting more and more desperate. I heard voices coming up the stairs and the footfall of what could have been up to about 10 people. Two doors left. I tried the first and it opened. I swept quickly inside and closed it behind me. There was no way of locking it so I quickly located the door wedge usually used to keep it open and kicked it as hard as I could in an attempt to keep the door shut. I rushed across the classroom towards the big stationary cupboard, thankfully that too was open. I pushed up the bottom most shelf spilling the pens and other bits of stationary, which were on it and climbed inside and assumed a very cramped fetal position. I reached out and pulled the 2 doors shut and hoped for the best.

As I waited there I could hear the group of feet coming loudly down the corridor. They were jeering and shouting and I could hear them trying door handles as they went. Then, they were outside. I heard the door handle shake and what must have been the palm of someone's hand slap against the window. "This one's locked too!" Someone shouted. It all went quite. It all went horribly quite for about 5 minutes. Which in real time is nothing, but in sitting scared in a cupboard in fetal position time, is about 4 years. I dare not breathe, I dare not move, I just waited.

The door burst open with a loud bang. I froze preparing for the worst. I heard someone enter the room, just one person. It was definitely just one set of footsteps. A big clang rang out from near the entrance to the room; whoever had come in must have kicked the wedge I had lodged into place across the room and onto a metal chair leg. The footsteps moved around the room, one way and then another. Then they came closer. The footsteps came right up to the cupboard door and stopped. This was it. 10 verses 1, no chance. But 1 verses 1, a good chance I thought (even if it is the giant ginger tosser's brother!)

I made my decision that attack is far better than defense (obviously going against all my prior, yet meager martial arts teachings) and leapt out of the cupboard jumping straight onto the figure that was looking the other way across the room. I pulled my right tightly clenched fist back ready to strike and bundled into the figure. As soon as I made contact I realized that it wasn't in fact one of Todd's gang, it was actually Gary Clearly, one of the premises team at the school, I lowered my fist and got to my feet sharpish and started to bring my heart rate back to just a mild gallop,

Poor Gary didn't know what on Earth was going on, "What the hell do you think you are doing!!?" He said, "You frightened the living piss out of me!"

I apologised profusely and explained the situation in detail to him. "I know." He continued, "I have just chased 3 of them out of the Math's block, they have smashed a door downstairs and have turned a number of classrooms upside down, what do they want with you?" Again I explained the situation I had gotten myself into. I explained about my 'relationship' with Todd and about the incident with the 'ginger tosser'.

"I am afraid Matt, I am going to have to report this." I agreed with him. Looks like I will need all the help I can get at the moment, this could have been a very nasty situation with a very painful ending. Gary called my dad from his mobile and he reluctantly came and picked me up, although it did take him nearly an hour to travel the 5 mins down the road.

Dad arrived; I thanked Gary for his help and jumped in the car. "What the hell have you done now?" Asked Dad, "What are you getting yourself mixed up with that lot for? I bet its over that bloody girl isn't it?"

I explained myself yet again and unusually for my Dad, he swallowed it first time. No questions, no doubts, nothing. Just a brief nod of the head and a quiet 5 minute journey home.

Once home he made me a cup of tea and sat down with me in the lounge and began:

"Listen Matt, I know that this situation is not one that you have deliberately created, but things are going to have to change a little over the next few weeks. I see these guys around a lot and you are really going to have to watch yourself around them. Particularly that Todd character you mentioned, his family are mad and he is no different. I am pretty sure you can fight and look after yourself, but there are a lot of them and god knows what they could be carrying around with them. If something would happen to you we would all be crushed, we love you you know. So from Monday, I will drop you and Martin at school and pick you up at the end. That way you won't have to go through this again and I will know you are safe." I agreed with him and thanked him for understanding. It's not a bad idea considering what has happened today, I don't really want to go through that again.

I rang Sasha and explained what had happened yet again. She apologised for not being at the gates, she explained that she was held up by her English teacher to finish off a piece of coursework. I explained that I was glad that she wasn't with me, as the stationary cupboard would never have been able to fit us both. My dad popped his head around my bedroom door while I was on the phone to Sasha and said, "Matt, why don't you invite her around for dinner tomorrow night? Say 6 o' clock? Mum and I would really like to meet her."

I did, she agreed. God knows what we have just gotten ourselves into. I am not sure that this is the best of ideas, but it's done now.

Oh god. At least we don't have a cat.

## Saturday, March 4th

Oh my god, my parents are a fucking hideous embarrassment! Sasha arrived for dinner at around 17:45 and left at 20.56. I know this almost to the second as I was in severe psychological pain for the duration of her stay. Now don't get me wrong dear diary, if my parents were not around the 3 hours and 38 minutes would have passed in what seemed like a blink of the eye. But with my parents present the same amount of time seemed to last just shy of 46 weeks.

My dad decided to turn into the worlds shittest stand up comedian. Here are a few of the priceless gems he decided to share with my beloved Sasha:

My father used to walk up and down the catwalks of Paris, Milan and Madrid carrying a bag of sesame seed buns. He was a fantastic 'role model'

I took my wife to the races the other day and she got stung 5 times on her head. She really had a bee in her bonnet.

The other day my wife said to me "Dum de dum." I said, "pardon?" She then said, "La de da." I said, "Well you've changed your tune.

You see, an absolute bag of shit.

My mum spent the evening showing Sasha pictures of me when I was a toddler. I honestly had no idea that there were so many pictures of me with my cock and/or ass on display in circulation. I am tempted to write a letter to the company that has developed them and ask them why they felt it appropriate to print so many pictures of a 2-year-old child fully displaying his rather small and inoffensive family jewels! It really doesn't seem right at all, I thought this country was supposed to be clamping down on pedophiles.

What made it worse, was that Sasha spent the whole of her time at my house laughing at my dad's shit jokes and the several thousand pictures of my pre-pubescent balls. Nice. One things for sure though, my parents absolutely fell head over heels for Sasha, and why shouldn't they – she is completely perfect. As embarrassed as I was with the situation I couldn't help smile as Sasha's face lit up every time she laughed. She is gorgeous when all of the time to me, but when she laughs her whole body laughs. She glows and I love her more.

My mum was relentless, photo after photo, story after story, bollock after bollock. But Sasha just carried on laughing and genuinely seemed interested in everything the crazy woman had to say. She really must be into me

The only saving grace of the whole evening was the fact that my dad cooked instead of my mum. My mum cooking may well have spelt the end for Sasha and I, so thank the lord!

Credit where credit is due, my dad pulled it out of the bag as far as diner was concerned. We had a rocket salad with caramelised onion and crispy streaky bacon for starter. Followed by filet steak with a peppercorn sauce. For desert he made Eton mess, which was just out of this world.

I walked Sasha back home after the meal; she had a beaming smile on her face all the way home. We laughed and repeated some of my dad's shit jokes. We got to her door and kissed for what seemed a lifetime. And then she said, "Matt, I am just so happy I have you. I really love you. I hope you know that. I mean, I know we haven't been seeing each other that long, but this just feels so right. I hope that doesn't scare you."

Her words warmed me right through to the bone, which was quite impressive as it was a bloody freezing evening! I pulled her close and kissed her tenderly and looked her in the eyes deeply and said, "I am head over heels in love with you and the only thing that scares me is the thought that at some point in the future I may not have you. I really do love you too."

"You are stuck with me forever!" She said
"Fine by me." I said coolly and shrugged my shoulders, kissed her on the cheek and turned for home.

Man, I really am in love. That's a really good thing.

## Sunday, March 5th

Sasha and I have agreed that we are indeed going to go camping. Martin has also agreed to come, along with Sasha's best friend Dawn Frost. Sasha seems to think that they are a match made in heaven. I don't think Martin has ever actually had a girlfriend before, in fact I actually think girls scare him a bit. Girls are not really a topic of conversation for Martin and I; we mainly talk about video games, TV, films and music. I think the only time we drift into the 'girl' topic is when a hot girl passes us by in the street and one of us (usually me actually!) says something sexist, such as: "Look at the fun bags on that!" Or, "I would absolutely destroy her!" That kind of thing, not exactly Keats or Byron.

I popped around Nan's with the family to reluctantly receive a warm pound pressed into my hand and an itchy, hairy kiss. It was nice to see her though, she does make me chuckle with her funny ways. I particularly like the way he announces to the whole street whenever she decides she needs to use the loo. "Just off to the little girls room to do a wee wee!" Or,

"Just popping to the loo, will be a while…..its numbers twos!" And with that off she waddles like a drunken duck with a hunchback.

All in all this has been a pretty action packed weekend, so much so that I had almost forgotten about the incident on Friday. I rang Martin and explained the whole chauffer situation, with my Dad embarrassingly taking us to and from school like a couple of 5-year-old twats.

"No worries" said Martin, "Saves walking and being beaten up."

A good point.

**Monday, March 6th**

Day one of operation 'School Run'. I'm not sure I can take much more of the sniggering and finger pointing from the overly judgmental general school population. The drive to school was actually fine. In fact, I would happily be driven to school every day, especially on freezing cold mornings like todays was. But to be picked up at the end of the day is just hideously embarrassing. To make matters worse, my dad has decided that he would not only park right as close as possible to the school gates, but would also stand next to the car, leaning on it in some kind of homage to a 70's catalogue model, thankfully minus the driving gloves. I didn't fancy Sasha having to walk home on her own, so offered her a lift too, I was certain that dad wouldn't mind.

It was a good job that he was there however as Todd and his gang of assholes had again decided to show up. Had he not been there I am certain that I would have received an almighty kicking, there were at least 6 of them including the ginger tossers brother. Todd obviously couldn't resist shouting something, and said. "Need daddy to come and pick you up do you, you fucking faggot!?" I smiled, waved and got in the car with Martin and Sasha. My dad turned the car and pulled up right next to where Todd and assholes were, wound down his window and said, "Daddy will be picking Matt up. And daddy will take a fucking bat to your thick skull if you come anywhere near my boy again!" Fair play dad, I really didn't know that you had that in you! He sounded so much like a rough east end gangster (even if he was wearing brown cords and a yellow check shirt), that Todd and his merry men were left speechless. They certainly didn't expect that. My dad apologised to us all for his bad language as we drove off.

I brought up the topic of my friends and I going camping next weekend, it went down with mixed feelings from the olds. Mum was happy with it and actually thought it was a good idea (pretty sure she just wants me out of the house for a couple of days). But my dad was dead against it. He seems to think that we are going to go away on some kind of sordid camping orgy, where everyone will get stabbed, hooked on heroin and return home pregnant.

It's not a clear yes as yet, but that didn't stop Sasha, Martin and I from planning it online. The plan so far:

Friday: As soon as the school bell goes we leg it down to Worthing station and get the train to Hassocks. Once we arrive at Hassock (about 20 mins on the train) we need to walk about 2 to 3 miles (to save money) to the campsite. We have chosen to go to the 'Happy Jack' campsite which is just outside of Ditchling. We have chosen this camp site for 2 main reasons:

1) it's cheap (£6 per tent per night – bargain!)

2) They provide you with sectioned off community areas with a fire pit and logs (at a small extra cost).

Once we have pitched our tents, we will then source an off-license naive enough to supply us with copious amounts of cheap yet strong alcohol. The last part of the plan is pretty straight forward. Return to the campsite, light a fire and slip into alcohol induced comas.

Saturday: Wake up late (probably around 12pm); take some painkillers for the very likely hangover I predict. Attempt to have sex with Sasha and then get up and sort out a communal breakfast.

For Saturday after lunch we have decided that we are all going to go fishing at Brighton Marina, Martin knows a man that hires out fishing kit at a reasonable price at the marina. He goes fishing a lot with his dad and claims to know what he is doing. The idea is that we catch a bunch of fish and cook them on the campfire Saturday evening when we return, but I am pretty certain that we will catch bugger all and have to buy some sausages and burgers on the way back. Should be fun though.

I imagine that we will be drinking a lot less alcohol on the Saturday evening and I am hoping that Sasha and I can have an early night and spend a little 'quality' time together. Neither of us has proved particularly vocal during our love making so far, so I am certain that the privacy that a thin sheet of nylon allows will be sufficient for our very basic needs.

Sunday: After breakfast we are going to pretty much pack up and head off home, getting the train from Hassocks back to Worthing.

The number of people coming on our camping trip has now increased, confirmed attendees are:

Me - (Although my dad has technically not said yes as yet)
Sasha – Love of my life
Martin – Best chum
Dawn Frost – Sasha's best friend, who we hope will fall in love with Martin over the weekend
Jack Simons – Nice kid from my year group who is quite friendly with Martin and in a number of his classes. His dad has also split from his mum and the

two of them with lonely dads in tow often catch up to go fishing and bowling etc.

Karen James – Karen is Dawns friend and is incredibly pretty, she is currently trying to find work as a model. Not a patch on Sasha however.

Bobby Larkin – A friend of Jack's who, to be fair to him is a bit of an annoying sod. He has ADHD and just cannot sit still for 2 minutes. Much as I sympathise with his condition, he really is a mighty pain in the arse and I wish he wasn't coming.

Nicola Parry – Another of Sasha's friends who I literally know nothing about other than the fact that she is in my year group, very quiet and has the biggest set of tits I have ever seen offline. In fact they are so big that we have affectionately named her, Nicola Melons.

Marie Richards – Yet another of Sasha's crew, who is in a number of my classes in school and is lovely. Best way to describe her is 'bubbly'. Needless to say she is a larger girl who is quite funny. I know she will be staying in a tent with Nicola and only hope that they have one large enough that will be able to contain the large volume of boobs and arse on offer.

So that's the camping party. Sasha and I in my tent. Martin, Jack and bobby in Martins tent. Dawn and Karen together and Nicola and Marie with all their wobbly bits in theirs. 4 tents in total, should be really fun.

Note to self: Must buy condoms and check my dad's old tent and sleeping bag.

## Tuesday, March 7th

Quite surprised to see that Todd and gang were not at the gates today, perhaps my dad's threats have gotten to them and they have decided that attacking me is not such a wise move anymore, given that my dad is the reincarnation of both Kray's and would take a 'bat to their skulls'.

It would have been my Granddad's birthday today, so we went straight from school dropped off Sasha and Martin and picked up my mum, brother and nan and headed off to the cemetery. It was a bit of a squash in the car, especially as I had to sit in the back with my mum and brother while my Nan had the front seat. Given that I am the biggest, surely that should mean I have automatic rights to the front seat, my Nan is quite literally the size of a hobbit, and a malnourished one at that.

I hate cemeteries, I think it's because they force you to face your inevitable demise. Although I am still young I do think about this quite a lot and it does really bother me. In many ways I wish I had a faith, at least it would provide my mind with some kind of focus and stop me from stewing on the issue. I really do respect people who have a faith, to be able to throw yourself completely at something you believe 100% must not only be comforting, but fulfilling. My family are what I would term 'faith ignorers'. Religion is not a topic of conversation in our house, ever. Neither my mum nor dad were brought up with any religious input in exactly the same way as myself.

Conversations in my house which deal with death tend to be focused around age and 'fairness'. The too common statements that are spoken are:

- For an old person dying: "Well, they had a good innings."
- For a young person dying: "Tragic, that's no age."

So, I guess I have grown up spiritually ignorant and that is why death scares me.

At the graveyard Nan arranged some flowers she had brought along with her and we all stood around and exchanged funny stories about my Granddad. My dad (the son of my Granddad by the way), told the following story:

"I remember one summer, when my dad was a younger man, around 27 or 28 and I was a 6 year old, I remember him taking mum and me to the seaside. We lived in Hampshire at the time, just south of Reading and travelled down to Bournemouth for the day. We set off early in my dad's old Ford and arrived at around 10am. We had a great day on the beach, building sandcastles and burying dad. At lunchtime we popped up into the town and had something to eat, I have no idea what mum and I had, but he certainly had a bowl of muscles. To say that the muscles disagreed with him is an understatement. We head off back home at around 5 o'clock and had what I can only describe as one of the most eventful journeys I have ever been on. About 30 minutes into the journey home, it began. My dad started to complain that he was feeling unwell and started sweating quite profusely. He then demanded that we open all of the windows in the car to cool him down. Then he threw up. I have never seen projectile vomiting of that caliber before or since. The vomit left his mouth, travelled straight over the steering wheel and crashed like a wave all across the dashboard and windscreen. It was bright yellow vomit full of muscly lumps and connective tissue that instantly stunk out the car with the smell of rotting fish and bile. The smell was so bad that my mum threw up instantly, filling the left hand side of the dashboard with a more traditionally watery brown quantity of vomit. Naturally, I followed suit seconds later and covered myself in sick. Dad's view out of the window was pretty obscured by now given the greasy muscle juice mosaic he had just created and he was obviously still feeling quite queasy too. He decided that he would leave the A road we were on a.s.a.p. I remember him even trying the windscreen wipers to try and clear the view! He threw up 2 more times before we got to a service station and literally sprinted as fast as he could to the toilets and avoided soiling his pants by milliseconds. The bowl of muscles were obviously not overly happy with the whole being eaten deal and were determined to break out of his body through every opening. It took mum and dad over an hour to clear the wind screen and dashboard and 2 more visits to the toilets before we head back home."

Dad's story really did lift everyone's mood and we all stood at the faded gravestone with big smiles on our faces (including my nan) for 5 minutes or so before heading back to the car and going home.

I listened to cemetery gates again this evening, still with a smile on my face from dad's story. It's a sad state of affairs this death business, but it's great to remember those who have passed in a positive way. Then again, we won't always visit the grave. When we have all passed away, there will be nobody to visit him and that's a sad thought. That will happen to all of us I guess, the only answer I suppose is to make the most of the time you have and pay no mind to it. After all there is not a lot you can do about it.

I think a couple of episodes of Red Dwarf are in order to cheer me up.

## Wednesday, March 8th

Finally my dad has actually consented to my going camping this Friday, which is a result, as I would have looked a complete plank pulling out now!

I checked on the kit when I got home from school today and it all seems pretty ship shape to me, apart from the sleeping bag which I have given to mum to dry clean for me. The weather forecast claims that it will be cold but dry, which is a bit of a result too. I am not too sure when my dad last used his tent. It was probably when he was the same age as I am now. We have never been camping together as a family.

We either go to Malaga in the South of Spain, or nowhere. The only time we actually do go on holiday is when my dad receives a good bonus from work and there is nothing drastic that needs doing in the house. All in all I can really only recollect 5 holidays that we have been on.

In school I was called to my head of years office (Mrs. Pearce) and given a bit of a telling off about my 'public displays of affection' with Sasha. I kind of agree with her in all honesty and agreed to calm things down a little. I explained the warning to Sasha, but she just said, "I guess we will just have to be a little more discreet. I will meet you behind the boiler room at lunchtime." Dear diary, I cannot explain just what happened behind the boiler room at lunchtime, but let's just say that     Mrs. Pearce certainly would not have approved.

I have spent my evening revising. I really seem to be getting on top of things at school at the moment and I am starting to even feel quite confident about the exams coming up in May and June. I have been thinking more seriously about going to sixth form in September; I just need to make a decision about what I am going to do. I am currently considering doing Chemistry and Biology, as I seem to be doing particularly well in these subjects. Definitely not Physics though, I find that bloody difficult. I enjoy Geography and I am getting a lot better at English too (although I am sure my writing in this diary leaves a lot to be desired! I certainly wouldn't hand it into my English teacher for marking that's for sure!)

As for a career, I still have no idea what I would like to do.

**Thursday, March 9th**

It's a good job that Dad picked me up today as Todd and his gang of prepubescent toss bags were waiting at the school gates again, no doubt with the same intention of giving me a damn good kicking. They hurled the obvious abuse at Martin, Sasha and I, but this time my dad even managed to get a special mention. They had obviously 'braved up' a little since his well-made threats on Monday. My dad however, didn't rise to it, just drove off ignoring the pack of twats.

Truth be told I am getting a little nervous about setting off on the camping trip tomorrow. What if those tossers are there when we try to make it to the station? Probably for the best if I arrange it with dad to pick me, Sasha and Martin up at the gates and drop us at the station where we can wait for the others. Yes definitely a good idea.

I have spent the evening packing things ready for tomorrow.

Tent – Check
Rucksack full of jeans warm tops and my least thread bear boxer shorts – check
Camping stove with gas bottles – check

Freshly dry cleaned sleeping bag – check
Toothbrush, toothpaste and shower gel – check
Cash - check
1 Packet of ribbed Johnnies (for her pleasure) – check
(the most important item)


**Friday, March 10th**

As soon at the bell went for the end of the day I was out of my chair and off like a rocket. I met Sasha and Martin at the gates and helped bundle their stuff into dads waiting car. Mine was already in there from when I packed it the previous night. As we drove off and turned the corner out of the school drive Todd and his cling-ons were walking to their usual place to hang out, no doubt on the off chance of my being there alone to give me a damn good kicking. A relief that dad picked us up, we would have definitely bumped into them if we had tried to make it on our own.

That said, this was my first time camping and I was very excited. My only snagging doubt was whether my dad's ancient tent was still functional. Rain wasn't forecast, but as anyone who lives on this fair island of ours knows – that can change in a millisecond. It would be a right pain in the arse if we got washed out on the first night and had to pack up and go home.

We jumped out of dad's car at the station and it was only then that the walk from Hassocks to Ditchling seemed very unlikely, I had packed far too much! We all agreed at that point that a little investment in a cab to the campsite would be very wise. My dad found just enough time to take me to one side and give me a final lecture about sensible drinking, safe sex and class A drugs before heading off home. I felt free, freer in fact than I have ever done before.

The others all arrived about 30 minutes later minus Bobby. We waited another 10 minutes and then as it was cold decided to head across the road and have a coffee in the coffee shop. Another 30 mins went by and still nothing. Martin tried calling him a couple of times on his mobile, but there was no answer. We discussed what to do and voted unanimously to just head off without him.

We arrived at Hassocks station just after 6:00pm and divided ourselves into 3 cabs, cheeky buggers would not take 5 in one and 4 in another, I'm sure they must be allowed to do that and it was just a scam to get more cash out of us. We stopped at an off license on the way and sent Jack in alone as he not only looked the oldest, but also had a great fake id. Several large bags of alcoholic produce later we headed off again.

When we arrived at the campsite it was already getting quite dark and getting the tents pitched using the one torch Martin had thoughtfully brought along was a major pain in the arse. It took us the best part of 2 hours to construct a rather amateur set of tents and get the fire going, which was a relief as by the time we had finished pitching the temperature had dropped right down to near freezing point.

Sitting around the campfire was amazing. We were all so cold that we all got into our sleeping bags and parked ourselves around the fire, only taking out our arms to take a drink of the rather dodgy concoction of drinks Jack had decided to buy. Martin took it upon himself to keep the fire burning bright deep into the early hours of the morning.

As the surroundings were dark and very spooky we obviously took turns telling the scariest ghost stories we could. Sasha cuddled into me as Jack told us his one:

"A man called Peter Hayward was trekking along the South Downs way alone from Eastbourne all the way to Winchester. He set off from Eastbourne in the morning and planned to reach a campsite just the other side of Worthing in the evening, completing the 80 mile trek the following day. All was fine as he set off, it was February however and the sun was hidden really well behind the dense black clouds that threatened to open up at any moment. The downs path was completely empty, it wasn't until he reached just south of Lewes that he came across another soul. The shape of a person came into view as he began the decent of a steep hill. The person appeared to be sitting. As he walked closer the shape began to focus. It was a man. It was a man in his mid-twenties. He was rocking with his hands crossed across his chest.

He was only wearing a white T shirt and light linen trousers.
As Peter drew closer he noticed that the man in his mid-twenties was staring straight at him, his head tilted back as he rocked with a weird and eerie smile spread across his face. Peters heart race went through the roof, this just felt wrong. Something felt very wrong.

As he drew level with the man he increased his pace and his eyes ahead trying desperately not to look. But the urge to look was too great.

The man had started to rise from the bench, his lips pulled back revealing a set jagged teeth covered in what appeared to be blood. His mouth fell open as he stood fully upright and he let out an almighty screeching scream that boomed out across the downs and made Peter jump straight out of his skin. He allowed himself to panic and burst immediately into a run. He was still heading down hill and quickly reached a very quick pace, too quick. His feet tangled and he lost his footing and he fell forwards. Over and over he went for a good 20 seconds until he came to a rest. Ignoring the cuts and scrapes he leaped immediately back to his feet and looked back. There was nothing. The bench where the man had been was empty. He was alone again.

He composed himself and began walking quickly. As he walked he began to assess the injuries he had sustained in his fall. He was bleeding from the nose and from a cut above his left eye, both his knees were stinging and he could not move 3 of the fingers on his left hand. He was pretty certain that he had broken them. He decided that he needed to seek some treatment so headed south and into Brighton. He reached the Royal Sussex early evening and waited in accident and emergency to be seen. After a 2 hour wait he was seen by the triage nurse who booked him in for an x-ray on the suspected broken fingers. He went through to the x-ray waiting room, took off his coat and placed his back pack on the plastic chairs and went through to the toilet to clean up a little.

The warm water felt great in his hands. He ducked his head and splashed the water over his face. He stood and froze.

The man was stood behind him. He reached forward and grabbed Peters chin with icy fingers lifting his head up and with his other he slowly but powerfully dragged a barber's razor deep through the front of his throat. The last thing Peter saw as the blood flooded out of his open neck was the man leaning forwards, sinking his teeth into the side of his face. Then nothing."

We were all silent. I think the story knocked us all for six!

Then Martin said, "I remember reading about that." We all looked straight at Martin horrified.

"What are you talking about?" Sasha asked.

"It was about two years ago," Martin continued "A back packer was found murdered in the Royal Sussex. His throat was slashed and he had a huge bite mark on the side of his face. If you don't believe me google it."

"I thought it was just a story." Said Jack, "my dad told it to me."
Fortunately none of the smart phone owners had enough of a signal to be able to confirm the horrible story, which was a good thing as I am not too sure that I would have been able to sleep knowing there was a jagged toothed razor wielding murdered on the loose in the South Downs.

As the fire died down we all retreated to our tents and Sasha and I fell asleep in each other's arms


### Saturday, March 11th

Well to say that today didn't go according to plan is an understatement. The early morning tent sex was amazing, the communal campfire breakfast was lovely, the day out fishing was as unproductive as I predicted, but fine. But the evening was anything but fine and certainly not something I had predicted.

We arrived back at the campsite after our rather fruitless fishing expedition to find a scene of absolute carnage. All of the tents had been slashed and raised to the ground. The rucks sacks and sleeping bags had been scattered all around the clearing and some of them were still smoldering from where they had been placed on the fire earlier. There was a strong smell of urine from the area, which suggested to me that whoever had done this had clearly decided that slashing and burning was just not enough and that pissing over the remains was also essential.

Who though? Well, that was just about to become very clear.

As we started the lengthy clean-up process and sent Dawn and Karen off to get a pack of black bin liners from the same off license that we popped into on the Friday evening, Todd followed by 5 of his friends walked into the clearing.

My heart stopped. I found out later in the day that the reason that Bobby hadn't managed to join us was because he had been intercepted by Todd and his goons on the way to the station. Apparently they managed to drag him down a lane and beat several shades of shit out of him until he confessed to where the camping expedition was heading and exactly who was going to be there, Christ knows how he found out we were going camping. So there they were.

"We have unfinished business." Said Todd very menacingly to me. He reached into his jacket pocket and pulled out a huge knife. My heart went from stationary to about 200bpm in a second. I reached down to the ground while maintaining eye contact with Todd and picked up a steel tent pole with a nice pointy end. I definitely wasn't planning on going down without a fight.

"Martin, get everyone out of here and get help." I said calmly. Martin said, "No, we are all staying with you." I shouted as loud as I could, "Get everyone out, and get Sasha away from here, now!" He got the point and started to reluctantly turn everyone away to leave. And so I was stood there, 1 verses 6. I didn't fancy my odds at all, especially against that knife. It was more of a machete that a knife and I knew that he was planning on using it.

We stood facing off for what in reality was probably only 10 second, but seemed like an ice age. And then it happened. The ginger tossers gigantic brother broke their line and lunged at me. I managed to shuffle left and put a decent front kick into his on leading right leg. He spun like a top and I whacked him hard with the pole across his ear and cheek as he dropped. He landed almost at my feet and I stamped on his jaw so hard that it took him out of the equation completely.

1 verses 5, still not great odds, but it was a start and certainly a lot better than a second ago I thought.

They all rushed me. I was definitely going to take a beating here, no 2 ways about it. But before they got to me I managed to land a stinging blow to Todd's hand making him drop the sword of a knife he had in his hand and recoil in pain. I got 1 decent punch in and a good kick to someone's knee before I was bundled to the ground. Once down the blows rained in, I was kicked punched stamped on, spat on but thankfully not stabbed. The last thing I remember was seeing one of them picking up my camping stove and coming towards me, raising it above their head. Then it went dark.

I woke up in Hayward's Heath hospital at around 9 o'clock in the evening with a pounding headache and blood all over my hands and T-shirt. Sasha and my mum were at my bedside and seemed over joyed that I had come around. Despite the headache and a few aches and pains I didn't actually feel that bad at all. The extent of my injuries:

- 1 concussion - check
- 1 severely bruised left eye - check
- 1 heavily bruised femur - check
- 1 bit of ligament damage in my left index finger (where they tried to peel my fingers away from my head to give me a bit more punishment I guess) - check
- 1 very bruised and sore back! - check

With all the kisses and cuddles I received from my mum and Sasha I almost received a few more lip and cheek injuries. The doctors have decided to keep me in overnight just to be on the safe side (apparently quite common after someone has played football with your head), but truth be told I feel pretty good considering what could have happened.

Mum popped off for a cup of tea and Sasha filled me in with the bits I missed. After I was knocked unconscious, Martin returned with the campsite owner and managed to stop the group from giving me an even more savage kicking. Martin had also called the police from his mobile and they arrived pretty sharpish by all accounts and arrested all 6 of the scumbags. Apparently the police brought Todd into Haywards Heath hospital too with a suspected fractured thumb. Ha ha, nice. 1 - 0 to me I'd say! I have nothing broken.

**Sunday, March 12th**

I was visited by the consultant just after a very runny scrambled egg breakfast and given the green light to go home. But why he felt the need to poke my thigh so hard I will never know, sadistic if you ask me.

Once home, getting up the stairs was interesting, but once I was in bed with a good dose of painkillers in me I felt just fine. Martin popped over after lunch and we watched a bit of crappy Sunday TV and reflected on the action packed Saturday. Sasha called round at around 2pm and Martin, not wanting to play gooseberry left us 'too it'. Dear diary, again I'm afraid I will have to spare you the details, but when Sasha left, I felt much better...... 'Twice'.

Sasha left at around 5 and I just about managed to finish my dinner before the police came around and took a statement from me. I gave them the blow-by-blow account and they seemed genuinely impressed by my bravery, but did comment that I should actually have 'legged it'. Let's just hope they throw the book at Todd and put him in a young offender's prison. It would be great to have him out of my hair for a little while so I can concentrate on my studies and maybe even go back and fore to school unchaperoned.

Other than that I have pretty much been stuck here in bed all day. The painkillers are quite strong and I am a little drowsy, but otherwise ok. I did actually want to go into school tomorrow, but it's a big no no from the folks. Hopefully I will be back in on Tuesday.

Ah well, back to my Red Dwarf novel for the 1000th time I suppose.


**Monday, March 13th**
I am bored to death. I have been lying in this bed for what now seems like weeks with nothing but shitty daytime TV for company. How anyone could cope with being unemployed is beyond me. If anything good has come out of this situation is that I am now more determined than ever to do well in this summer's exams and stay on in sixth form in September. That said, after the morning of drivel I have sat through I would now consider myself an expert in property development, antiques and seeking relatives of the recently deceased. Every cloud…

Sasha could not come around today as she has a load of coursework that needs finishing off, so the highlight of my day was a visit form Martin. Martin did however come armed with some pretty interesting news on the back of Saturday's events. Todd and his clan had indeed been arrested. They all spent a night in the cells for their days work. Martin seemed to think that they were all charged with a variety of things. Damaging property, violent conduct, disturbing the peace and a bunch of other things I have never heard of. He had even heard from one person that Todd was being charged with ABH and was caught in possession of a deadly weapon. Now that would be nice, surely he would go down for that!

I am feeling better again today and even managed to limp downstairs for my evening meal. The bruise on my leg is an absolute beauty and it does feel like I have a dead leg whenever I try to move it. But as I wanted to go into school tomorrow and avoid finding out what another bunch of irritating sods have in their attics, I had to show my parents that I was fully recovered. Thankfully my mum and dad agreed and seemed impressed that I actually wanted to go too.


### Tuesday, March 14$^{th}$

Other than it being a bit of a struggle getting in and out of dad's car and up and down stairs, today in school went pretty well. I was welcomed like a hero into my first lesson of the day. People clapping hands and pretending to bow down to me. I think the whole school has now had more than enough of Todd and his carrying on and they are just happy that someone decided to take a stand. Nice being a hero for a day though.

I am now well and truly sick of telling the story of what happened on Saturday. It's nice that people care and I appreciate that they want to know the exciting ins and outs, but enough is enough. I have now shortened my story to, "I was jumped, but managed to get a couple of hits in." That seems to get the message across and prevents a fleet of overly enquiring questions.

Word around the playground today was that Todd had been released from the police station yesterday evening. And some were even saying that he has only received a caution! Now, I find that very hard to believe considering the bloody great knife he was waving around. I would be not only astonished, but gutted if that is the case.

When I got home from school my dad led me into the living room and pointed at the sofa. He had laid out a whole new bunch of camping equipment. He said, "I figured you may want to give camping another bash when you feel up to it. Hopefully next time it will be a lot less traumatic." What an absolute legend! For the first time since I was about 6 I gave my dad a big hug and a kiss and said "Thank you!" and really meant it. I put the kit away carefully in the shed and went up for an early night.

So I have a new tent, sleeping bag, torch and camping stove. Let's just hope nobody decides to club me across the head with this one!

## Wednesday, March 15th

I am healing pretty quickly, the swelling in my eye is going down, it's a lovely rainbow colour though. My back is less bruised and my leg is feeling much less 'dead' than it did.

I walked past the ginger tosser and some of his friends in the Math's corridor today. I steadied myself for a bit of grief, but thankfully they gave me a bit of a wide birth. After they passed me, the ginger tosser obviously feeling a little bit braver decided to shout back down the corridor at me. "You were fucking lucky at the weekend! Todd is out now and he is gonna fucking stab you right up!" I turned round, smiled, waved and said, "nice!"

I have a bad feeling that this really isn't going to end well. This guy has it in for me big time and I really don't think he will rest until he has done me some serious damage.

When dad picked us up today he was there again. This time he was there alone and stooped down low to stare at me as we drove by dragging his finger across his neck with a weird look on his face. He really is starting to get to me now; I am starting to get worried. Sasha and Martin did their best to make me feel better on the way home, but it is all I can think about at the moment. Saturday was a close call in many respects, but I know damn well that Todd would not be satisfied with that. I'm pretty sure he wants me dead and will not stop until that is the case.

### Thursday, March 16<sup>th</sup>

I stayed at home today. I wasn't feeling particularly unwell, but really felt I needed a break from it all. Yesterday's encounter with Todd really spooked me out; and I think it may be a good idea to give school a miss for a bit, at least until after the weekend.

So today I achieved nothing apart from playing video games and watching crappy daytime TV. The highlight of the day was the cheese on toast my mum made me when she popped back home at lunch time.

It's just gone 7 o'clock and I have been called down for dinner 3 times now, but I think I am just going to curl up and go to sleep.

### Friday, March 17<sup>th</sup>

I stayed home from school again today. I stayed in bed until lunchtime when thankfully Sasha came around. I am that fed up at the moment that we didn't even do some of the great stuff that we usually do when we are alone. We kind of both just sat and cuddled, starring mindlessly at the TV, I can't even remember what we were watching. She didn't give me a hard time or anything, just a really sweet passionate kiss when she got up to leave for school and said, "You are taking me out on a date tomorrow night. To a comedy club in Brighton. We both need a night out away from it I think." I agreed, she blew me a kiss and was gone.

I managed to make it down for dinner this evening, dad cooked spaghetti Bolognese, which is one of my favorites. As we were finishing off dinner our atypically political conversation about whether we should have been looking for weapons of mass destruction in Iraq came to a shuddering halt as an almighty crash rang out from the lounge. We all sprang up out of our seats and ran the 15 or so paces into the longue to see a brick on the beige carpet surrounded by thousands of tiny shards of glass.

My dad was off like a greyhound and sprang down the corridor and out of the front door. My mum and I began sweeping up the mess and carefully bagged up the brick in a freezer bag in case the police wanted it for fingerprints.

My dad came back after 30 minutes or so and said, "The little shits were on bikes, I didn't catch a look at them, but I bet that fucking little tosser Todd is behind this. How the hell has he got our address?" I didn't much like the tone of his voice, it sounded as if he was almost accusing me of giving it to him. "I don't doubt it was him for a second, I have no idea where he has got it from though, he probably threatened to beat someone up for it, or worse knowing him." I rang Sasha and Martin to make sure they were ok, not that I suspected either of them of revealing my address, but figured that if he really wanted to know where I lived that badly either of them might have proved a good place to start. Both were fine and neither had seen Todd all day. Sasha did tell me however that Bobby was back in school today after the kicking he received from Todd and his merry men. I bet that is where he has got my address from.

Dad called the police, and to be fair to them, they were round in about 5 minutes. We explained the situation and who we suspected, they wrote down a few notes, took the bagged up brick and left.

After things had calmed down a little and we had managed to cover the broken window over with an elaborate series of black bin liners I asked my dad if I could take Sasha out tomorrow to the comedy club. He agreed on the condition that he would take us and bring us back. To be fair, it seemed logical so I emailed Sasha and made plans to pick her up at around 7pm.

## Saturday, March 18th

The window fixing company came this morning, 8:00am on a Saturday is great service, but I still resent being forced awake at that time on a weekend by relentless hammering and the steady tinkle of falling shards of glass.

After we had all finished breakfast the 2 guys packed up and left with our window looking as good as new. My dad wasn't too happy as he had decided to pay for it out of his own pocket rather than put it through as an insurance claim. He said something about 'premiums going up' that I didn't rightly understand, but just politely nodded along. He just kept on moaning about it all morning, "Bloody little thug, nearly £300 he has cost me. Just wait until I see him around!" We all just ignored him and his empty threats.

My date with Sasha thankfully came and went without incident. We did however have a great evening of laughing, kissing and cuddling.

It was the first time I have been to a comedy club and certainly not the last. 3 comedians and a compere who were all absolutely brilliant. Sasha and I laughed so much that at times we had trouble breathing. Exactly the tonic we needed after what we have been through of late.

Sasha has invited me around for Sunday lunch tomorrow. I have accepted, but wish to god now that I hadn't. The last time I was invited to dinner it really did not go well at all. In fact I am surprised that I have been invited back at all.

This time I will have to make sure I don't step on any pets, swear or break the crockery.

### Sunday, March 19th

I arrived at Sasha's for Sunday lunch at 12:00 on the dot, precisely as instructed, I was very nervous. Sasha's mum opened the door and gave me a huge hug and said, "It's great to see you again Matt, come on in. But watch the cats tail this time." I laughed and immediately felt 150% better.

I really need not have worried at all, the afternoon went really well. The food was great, the company was great and completely relaxed. As it turns out Sasha's dad is a bit of a red Dwarf nerd just like me, so we spent a lot of the afternoon discussing favorite episodes and the books. He even went so far as to lend me a couple of books that Rob Grant had written solo, Fat and Incompetence (deliberately spelt that way dear diary). Sasha's mum pulled out my mum's party trick and dug out all of the most embarrassing baby pictures of Sasha. I have to say, I am certain Sasha's pictures are a lot more embarrassing than mine, for a start none of my pictures featured me in the middle of having a piss!

Dad picked me up around 4:00pm and my ribs are still hurting now from laughing so much over the weekend. I am definitely going to school tomorrow, this weekend has done me the world of good.

## Monday, March 20th

It was certainly good to be back in school again today, I never want to sit through daytime TV again. I spoke with Sasha about my 2 days off at lunchtime and how it was driving me mad and making me feel worse the longer I stayed away from everything. Sasha explained that she thought being around people was the healthiest way to deal with problems like mine. She said that locking yourself away you can end up in a bit of a downwards spiral of depression. She went on to explain that she had seen the effects that depression has first-hand when her dad lost his job a few years ago. She said, "He was out of work and the family was really struggling financially. His moods were getting darker and darker and he was drinking every day, often starting in the morning and then straight through. Some days he would just sit stare at nothing. He would shout at everyone, nobody could do anything right. At the depressions darkest point I didn't want to come home from school in case I found my dad dead, really scary times."

This had really shaken her and I think seeing me starting to lock myself away started to bring back some of these old feelings. I reassured her that I was fine and that I could never be unhappy whilst I had her. We ignored the head of years close proximity warnings and snuggled up for the rest of the lunch break.

I am slightly anxious about tomorrow as my dad has to go up to Birmingham for a training day with his company, so he won't be able to give me a lift in the morning or more worryingly pick me up afterwards.

I am not quite sure how I am going to deal with the after school situation tomorrow. Staying in the school library to do some revision at the end of the day is one option. Legging it straight out of the gates and through the lanes is another option. At the moment I am undecided. Sasha definitely thinks the library option is the best, but I am of the opinion of if they are there, they are there and why should I go out of my way to avoid them. I suppose that I could always order a taxi. I will sleep on it.

## Tuesday, March 21st

I killed someone today. I am too tired to write now, I will have to try and sleep a little first.

## Wednesday, March 22nd

Dear diary, I am not quite sure where to start begin with this one.

I am sat in a tent in the woods at the moment. It is 9:14am and it's very cold here in my sleeping bag. I didn't sleep very well at all last night, probably only around 2 and a half hours tops. I have had so much to try and get my head around. I suppose I should start from the beginning, if anything at least it will help to get things straight in my head:

An ordinary day to begin with. I met Martin in the morning and walked into school. We talked on the way into school about Newsnight which was on TV last night (quite intellectual for us I suppose), they were debating about whether it was right for Asian women to wear a hijabs in the workplace and school in Britain. I say live and let live, but Martin for some reason had a bee in his bonnet about this issue and cannot understand why they are allowed, I never had him down as a racist.

"Our women have to wear what their women wear in their country, so I don't see why they should be anything different and besides it's a security issue. Motorcyclists have to take off their helmets when they go into a shop, where's the difference?" I wasn't too sure I wanted to get into a big discussion on this, but I really didn't like Martins argument so we finally agreed to disagree on this one.

School was pretty normal for a Friday. One monotonous blur of 5 lessons with a typically bland packed lunch and break time sprinkled on top. And then home time. It's safe to say that home time was a lot different.

At the end of school I foolishly opted for the 'scarpering straight out of the gates and through the lanes' option and that was exactly where he was. The steady jog I had maintained since leaving the school gates stopped as I turned the corner and saw him. I was left with 2 choices:

1. Turn and run – Not a great choice given the fact that there was three of them and they all had bikes.
2. Walk past them with my head held high and hope for the best – Not a great choice either, but maybe the last encounter at the campsite would have left a doubt in the back of Todd's head that attacking me wasn't a great idea.

I chose option 2.

As I walked up the lane I did my best to try and avoid Todd's glare, but he was more than determined enough to ensure that something was going to happen. He was sat on a recycling bin with his mate Ryan drinking a can of Stella and smoking a cigarette. "Look at this fucking dickhead, bad lane to walk down mate, I'm gonna fucking shank you right up, I told you I'd fucking shank you!" I tried to keep my eyes down, and increased my speed a bit, to just get past him as quick as possible. My heart was thumping; I could feel the pulse in my neck and the taste of metal in my mouth. I thought about turning and running, but I couldn't, something was pushing me on, I didn't have to take this, I didn't have to be scared, I was not going to be bullied. I got within 5 meters of the pair of them and they jumped off of the bin and walked out into the lane as if to block my way.

"Look at me when I'm talking to you dick head!"

I glanced up at him and said "I don't want any trouble, just let me go by". The rage I had felt against Todd after he slapped Sasha had all gone, I just wanted out of this situation. It didn't feel right, there was something nastier about Todd if that's possible. I guessed that he had probably had a bit to drink and a few spliffs too, minimum. Who knows what this nutter was into?

He reached in his back pocket and pulled out a knife which he skillfully opened with a slick move of his thumb and I heard it click as it locked into place. His mate dropped back a step and laughed too hard, full of nerves.
I ached to get out of the lane, but I was rooted and my heart was beating so fast that I was starting to feel dizzy.
His hand clenched the knife tight and he opened up his posture, slouching and coiling as if to strike at any moment. I took a step back to make sure I was out of range.
"You best fuck off where you came from, you ain't getting past, I will stab your fucking eyes out."

Then it happened.
He made a fake step towards me as if to pretend to attack, I flinched and he turned and shot a laugh at Ryan. My nerves stopped and I attacked.

As he turned his head back to me I was on him. I smashed my left fist down on the hand holding the knife and punched him straight under the chin with my right fist. I heard his teeth rock together and panic glaze across his eyes. He started to rock back, off balance, and I kicked his stomach to send him to the ground. Ryan just looked in a trance and started backing away. I grabbed the knife stood my ground and waited.

Todd picked himself up and felt at his jaw. "You are a fucking dead man." He let out a scream and ran at me, fists raised, clenched and full of hate, his eyes burning. I stepped to my right and swung the knife at him.

It struck him in the left side of his neck. The blade must have been about 3 inches long, all of it went in.

I let go of the knife immediately with panic and realization of just how real things had become and what I had just done.

Todd slumped against the wall eyes and mouth wide open. Eyes searching everywhere but no noise.

Ryan ran.

Todd started flapping on the floor, but couldn't seem to move his arms. He inhaled sharply and held it. He started shaking and smacking his lips as if trying to taste something in the air. He began flapping again, but still no noise, no movement from his arms.

I stood unable to do anything but watch what I had done to him. I didn't mean to have done this.

Blood started to come out of Todd's mouth and he started to writhe about arching his neck backwards as if straining for breath. Air started bubbling out of the deep wound in his neck.

His lips started turning blue and the colour drained completely from his face. His eyes still darting around were completely bloodshot and bulging. His body rolled towards me and I stepped back. The groin of his jeans grew wet as he passed urine and I would guess from the smell that he had also just soiled himself as well. He started to regain movement in his right arm, his hand grabbed the knife and started to pull it out. Blood sprayed out from the hole he had created and he let go.

Then he stopped, and stayed stopped.

I ran. I didn't know where I was heading at first but I had to get away from that lane.

I would go to my house and come up with a plan was the idea that grew in my head as I ran. There was no way I was going to hang around and go to prison for killing Todd. I decided that I was going to do a runner. I could always hand myself in if I decided to, but I could not do the reverse.

I reached my house. I ran upstairs and pulled out my rucksack from the bottom of my wardrobe. I stuffed it with enough clothes for a couple of days, making sure there were plenty of jumpers and a fleece, underwear, some toiletries and a towel. I grabbed my wallet and ran into my parent's room where I found £30 in notes and some loose change on the floor. In the kitchen I picked up a few tins of beans and some microwave pasta and rice packets, I figure they would taste bad but would be edible none the less. I collected a tin opener and a lighter from the draw and filled up my water bottle I use for PE and headed out into the garden. I went out to the shed where I grabbed the tent, sleeping bag, torch and camping stove. Before leaving I ran upstairs picked up the Sony Vista (I figured that I could sell it if I was desperate) and headed out.

I decided that I had to get away from Worthing and away from people as soon as possible. The chances were that Ryan had already reported what had happened and that the police had already found the body and were very soon going to be looking for me. I walked fast, but not too fast, I didn't want to arouse too much suspicion. It was already strange enough that I had a full rucksack on my back walking through the streets of Worthing. I stuck to the lanes wherever possible, I wanted as few people as possible to see me.

I headed up through the park at Hill barn, past the golf course and up onto the South Downs. I figured that if I got out into the countryside then the minimum amount of people would see me. Luckily the pathway was very quiet. Two people were all I came across on my way to the top of the Cissbury ring. Each time I hid in the dense foliage to the side of the path until they passed by.

I got to the top of the hill and had to make a decision. East would take me towards Brighton and west towards Winchester. West was my decision as I figured there would be less people, it's away from the city and the population around the South Downs way had to by significantly smaller. I know that the New Forest is near Southampton which could provide me with a place to camp undetected until I had come to a clear decision about what I was going to do.

I set off west and walked as the sun came down with nobody around for miles. I started to think more clearly as my pulse started to drop. I began asking myself questions:

- What would happen if I turned around and handed myself in?
- Can I go to prison for this?
- Am I really guilty, or is this self-defense?
- What will Sasha think?
- What will my parents think?
- Will I see Sasha again?
- Will it be worse for me the longer I stay away?
- Could the police think someone else did it?
- Could I get away with denying I did it?

I had no answers, so I just kept walking.

I reached an area of trees just south off of the south down way path and decided that I would head into and set up camp for the night. I figured that it was as obscure an area as I could find and it was starting to get really dark.

I quickly pitched the tent and clambered inside with all of my earthly positions. I have never felt so alone, I have never been so scared. I lay down in my sleeping bag, still fully dressed and absolutely freezing and carried on thinking.

What a mess, it is amazing how a single moment can set up an entirely different future. I have no idea how I am going to deal with this. Things were going so well, I have an amazing girlfriend, a loving family, school is finally going well. I know what I should do, I should turn right around, and head back home and face the music. Who knows, the police may understand that I acted in self-defense. But what if they didn't? What if Ryan lied, what if I had to spend years in prison. I don't think I could cope with that. Like I said, I can always hand myself in….but once I do, that's that and it's out of my hands, forever.

Today I have decided just to stay put and keep a low profile, I had walked a fair distance yesterday evening. I had crossed the A24 and I am pretty sure I am just south of Amberley. I figured that I would have been on the news and probably on some papers this morning so I have pretty much sat in the tent for most of the day. Police would be looking for me, and this is a logical route out of Worthing. So logical that I took it. The police may have dogs and items of clothing from my house with my scent on. It was wise to stay put, I have found a really obscured dense bit of woods, and the chances of someone walking past me were very small. I have ventured out a couple of times to stretch my legs and back and covered the tent the best I could with fallen leaves and sticks to camouflage it the best I could. I tried eating one of the microwave rice's at lunch time, Uncle Bens Mexican rice. I have had it hot and it just passes for food, cold it's pretty much unbearable, like eating slimy gravel with a hint of chili. I am halfway through my supply of water so will probably need to try and get some tomorrow, but the more I think about it the more sense it makes to stay put here for a couple of days at least. I have checked my money situation and I have a grand total of £34.53 which is not too bad, but it's not going to last very long. Whatever I decide to do, I need to decide it very quickly.

God I miss Sasha, fuck knows what I'm going to do about this.

### Thursday, March 23rd

I have never wondered what it would be like to kill someone, it's never even crossed my mind. But now that I have done it, albeit by accident I am not too sure what to think. I don't feel guilty at the moment, but maybe that will change as time goes by. The way I look at it, is that he attacked me and he pulled the knife. The only mistake I think I made was actually picking up the knife, I should have kicked the knife and run. I should have not walked up the lane. I should have stayed in the library. I should have booked a taxi. I should, I should, I should.

I didn't sleep well last night to say the least. I have no camping mat, so the only thing separating my spinal cord from the ice cold earth is a tiny sheet of nylon and a pathetically thin summer sleeping bag.

I woke up every half an hour or so, either due to the relentless cold, pain in my back or through the series of disturbing dreams I was having. Thankfully none of my dreams were about Todd, but there was one I had a few times.

It started with me entering a huge hotel. I stood in the atrium and looked around, it was like a huge hive with tunnels swirling out of view at every height and direction. I knew where I was going, to my room. I took a tunnel and walked. The ancient art deco electric candles on the wall flickered as I continued, walking and walking. After a few minutes I arrived at my room and started to search myself for my key. I could not find it.

From inside the room I could hear a voice, I pressed my ear up to the door to hear more clearly. It was Sasha and she sounded distressed, maybe even gagged. "Sasha!" I screamed over and over, but the noise on the other side of the door had stopped.

I turned and ran back down the corridor to the atrium in hope of finding the reception and a replacement key, the candle lights flickered more and more. A

creak behind me made me spin around. The tunnel was closing in behind me, I turned again and sprinted. The tunnel behind was collapsing in on itself at great speed I felt wind rushing fast towards me pushing me back. I tried to run faster but the floor seemed sticky and it was getting more and more difficult, my legs ached.
I stumbled and fell forwards and the tunnel collapsed around my legs, quickly up to my hips, then chest. I awoke.

I am not much of an expert in dreams, but I am certain that this one symbolises my situation. I can't get back to what I had, what I love and the way ahead looks impossible. But the tunnel hasn't collapsed around me yet.

I spent most of the day in the tent trying to keep warm and out of the way. I really had picked a great spot, not one single person, or animal for that matter passed me. I heard no voices, nothing, just the occasional whistle of the wind around the tent or leaf gently hitting the top of the tent.

I dozed a lot, so much that I started to become quite disorientated. I regularly got out of the tent and stretched my legs and back, walking in close rings around the tent.

I wonder what's going on at home, what must they be thinking. How will they be coping? I'm sure that even my irritating little brother is missing me, I certainly miss him.

As the darkness drew in I finished my meal of unmicrowaved microwave pasta and settled down to allow sleep to take me away from this place. It certainly seemed that another sleepless night lay ahead.

### Friday, March 24<sup>th</sup>

Sometimes being right is not a good thing.
As soon as my head touched down on my folded up coat I started thinking about the story Jack had told on our eventful camping trip. Here I was, camped just off the South Downs way, easy prey for the uncaptured, cheek biting, throat slashing homicidal maniac that roams these very paths.

After a night of fighting back images of slashed throats, the cold and my reoccurring dream of the hotel and the tunnels I got up in the morning more tired than I did when I lay down to sleep.

I decided that I would walk again today and further decided that my initial plan of heading towards the New Forest was as good as any at the moment.

I packed up the tent and equipment and did my best to randomly distribute the leaves and sticks around the area, to ensure that it didn't look camped on. I set off again on the South Downs way towards Winchester.
I figured that once (or rather if) I get to Winchester I

would buy a map and a compass so I knew exactly where the hell I was going.

I walked just off the main path so I could dip out of view if I saw people ahead. I followed the path through fields, woodlands and long grass. The going was pretty slow, in part because of the terrain, but mainly because I was carrying so much stuff and my back hurt like a bugger from sleeping rough. As I walked I tried to clear my mind, I concentrated on the scenery and sound of the surroundings and my own breathing. Today was quite cold and for most of the morning I was producing long trains of mist in every exhale. Watching this flow forward and disappear sent me into a trance.

I crossed the A286 road that was signposted to Midhurst (which I think means I am about half way to Winchester). I have played golf with my dad in Midhurst a couple of time, I should point out that I am rubbish at golf and only ever play my dad, about 2 or 3 times a year. But as rubbish as I am, I always seem to beat him!! This winds him up no end, as he does have an overinflated opinion of his golfing ability. Fortunately the path was empty for the majority of the day, I only needed to 'vanish' on 2 occasions. I may have been spotted by a few cars as I crossed over the road, but a bloke carrying a back pack along the South Down way is very unlikely to stick out like a sore thumb.

Night was closing in so I decided to set up camp. I set up my tent as I had previously, in a small area of trees about 100 meters away from the path. I ate the last bit of pasta and rice I had saved and looked longingly at the few tins I had brought along with me, my kingdom for a tin opener (mine seems to have gone missing). I am absolutely starving and almost completely out of water now. I will definitely have to chance it tomorrow and visit a shop to stock up, I'm not looking forward to that.

The walking bits in the open air bits of my day are fine, although I do spend a lot of it just trying to blank my mind. The big problem is when I am alone and in my tent. I am going mad with boredom, It's a good job I am tired tonight though or I know my mind would again start to wander. I am scared, I really don't mind admitting that, of the dark of the loneliness, of the unknown, of the consequences to what I have done. The nights have been pitch black, but there is no hiding from your own mind.

### Saturday, March 25th

It must have been very cold last night as when I woke up this morning the inside of the tent and all my stuff was soaking. I have never been a big one for baths and showers, don't get me wrong I'm not a smelly lad. But I have always seen them as a bit of a pain in the ass, and a waste of my time. I would give anything now for a warm bubble bath and a cup of tea. If my soggy tent and clothes wasn't bad enough, it absolutely pissed down today. I am bound to get pneumonia or something else equally horrific which requires my needing medical attention. What the hell do I do then?

Bizarrely I am writing this in a bush in a park in the middle of Winchester!

I walked a fair ol' distance today (amazing when you consider just how much it rained) and my legs are now incredibly sore, particularly my knees. I suppose they hurt so much as I again spent much of my time walking off the path to avoid attention. I reached the outskirts of Winchester at about 6:30pm and it was already getting pretty dark. This was ideal, low light meant that I felt alright about walking in the streets (even if I did stand out a bit with my huge soggy rucksack and sleeping bag!). My first stop was a small newsagent; this was to be my first contact with another human since I set off from Worthing so I left my kit outside so I didn't attract too much attention or receive any awkward questions. I bought a 1.5 litre bottle of water, a newspaper (the sun - classy), a chicken sandwich and 5 mars bars. That all came to the princely sum of £5.20 (quite pricey I thought, especially given how shite the sandwich was!).
I needn't have feared being identified as the small Asian man behind the counter didn't even look me in the face and all I managed during the whole transaction was a croaky "Thanks".

I was still soaking and felt I needed to at least change and have a quick wash. I followed the signs to the train station which again was thankfully very quiet, washed and brushed my teeth in the sink and changed in a cubical. I instantly felt better and more relaxed, so relaxed that I even managed to have my first bowel movement since Thursday night! Before leaving the toilet I spent 10 minutes drying out the inside of my sleeping bag under the hand dryer.

God must have decided to give me a break today as nobody came in to use the toilet while I was there and it had even stopped raining when I left.

I wandered the streets aimlessly, as if looking for something but not knowing what it was. It was nice to walk past people again. I was nervous at first, but people are so preoccupied with their own lives that they don't really notice you. I walked down ordinary streets, streets like mine. I saw families sitting in front of the television and laughing, families like mine. I saw people getting out of cars, late home from work with tired but happy faces. Happy that they were home. I wish I was home. My little brother, mum and dad. I miss being moaned at. I miss home. I miss Sasha. I walked for a bit more to clear my head.

By the time I realized how dark it was it must have been approaching 9:30pm and I was getting very tired. I can't tell you how tempted I was to just spend some of my remaining money on a bed and breakfast! Saying that, I probably wouldn't have had enough anyway. Instead I found a big park completely surrounded by bushes and trees. I walked all the way around it until I found a dense looking area of bushes and crept in. I broke a few branches here and there and just managed to squeeze the tent in, albeit a bit wonky! I hung up my wet clothes out the front of the tent and have settled down. I would have to get up early tomorrow if I am not to be seen by too many people. Once I had settled down and climbed inside my sleeping bag I checked the newspaper I had bought using my torch (note to self, get more batteries). There was not one thing about me within it, that's good I suppose, at least I have not made the nationals. I will see if I can pick up a more local paper tomorrow.

As I have been laying here I have been thinking about leaving the UK. I have no passport with me, but it could be possible. I suppose I could head to France. God knows how, but I think I will start with a map and compass to get my bearings. I will have to risk being seen tomorrow and pick them up before I leave Winchester. Maybe I could stow away on a ferry, or even steal a boat. I will sleep on it.

I found it difficult to settle, so I decided to write a poem. I'm not much of a poet. But putting the words together like a jigsaw puzzle has helped.

*Far from me but held close within my soul*
*No pictures to calm just memories to hold*
*And hold fast to them I do when sleep finally takes*
*Upon clouds we meet until daylight awakes*
*The cruel words I've said and cold thoughts all untrue*
*A moment of madness has stripped me from you*
*But hope is a card that I wait long to receive*

*From a dealer unyielding I can but believe*
*That your faces I will see in a day not too far*
*Upon ground and not cloud in skies unfilled with stars*
*Decisions I've made have carried me away*
*In a half-life that I live on a path that I've laid*
*I cannot turn back and I cannot give in*
*To the black I've created and this sadness within*
*So it's hope that I cling to that wrongs will be right*
*And the aching will stop and my future seem bright*
*But for now I must tread ever away from your arms*
*Into a future uncertain with my past far behind*


## Sunday, March 26th

I woke up just after 6:00am still very tired and groggy, but at least I was dryer than the following morning. My throat was really sore and I had developed a rather nasty chesty cough with complimentary runny nose. I ate one of my mars bars and washed it down with a few healthy swigs of water, packed up and headed off in the direction I figured would lead to the town. The plan was to try and find a shop that would sell a map and compass, maybe a little more food too. I figured it would be best to leave early and scout around while the streets were empty. Then I could lay low and wait until the shops opened to avoid minimum contact with people, buy my map and compass and get the hell out of here (batteries…. I must remember batteries for the torch too).

I had bugger all idea where I was, nothing from last night looked familiar at all. I walked aimlessly for nearly an hour before I saw a sign for the station where I had my luxury spa the previous evening, I thought that would be near the shops at least and so set off in that direction. I walked for 20 minutes and came across a small high street with a small number of shops including a WH Smiths, perfect! I walked up to the door to see what time it was due to open. 8:30, could be worse. The time was approaching 7:15, so I decided to try and find somewhere to sit out of sight until then. I crossed the road, took a few paces left and froze.

BOY 16, STABBED TO DEATH IN AN ALLEYWAY.

This was the headline written on the bill board outside a small newsagent. My heart raced in my chest and I felt as if I was going to faint. I walked up to the newsagents and saw a pile of newspapers laying on the floor. They were bound and dated as today, it certainly appeared as if they had just been dropped off ready for sale. I could only read the front page, but it was enough. It said something to the effect of:

"A 16 year old boy was found dead in an alleyway in Worthing, Sussex on Tuesday 21$^{st}$ March. Police have not released details of the deceased as they are still trying to contact the late boys natural parents. Turn to page 6 for full story."

Holy fuck, what the hell was on page 6? Could they have put a picture of me on there? Surely not, if they had that could spell disaster and all the more reason to get out of this town before it fully wakes up. I added a copy of this paper to my mental shopping list and walked around the corner and into a narrow lane. I set my rucksack down in a doorway to someone's garden and rest my head on my sleeping bag and closed my eyes and thought about how I could get to France.

I was awoke with a jump by an old mangy Alsatian sniffing around my shoes, I checked my watch, and it was 8:55. I cursed my stupidity and jumped to my feet and headed back onto the high street to do my shopping.

The high street was thankfully very quiet, I counted 2 people and 1 car drive past me as I walked to WH Smiths. WH Smiths was empty as well, mainly filled with staff sleepily getting on with their morning chores. I quickly set to work looking for the items on my mental shopping list. I headed straight for the books and quickly located the map section. I found a rough guide to France and flicked through it. It was exactly what I was after, full of maps and useful information. My second task was to find a map of the south that included the new forest and Southampton. There was nothing useful in the map area, just a few maps for hikers. I thought I would have a wander around and see if I could find my compass and batteries. I walked to the end of the isle and saw an ordinance survey map stand, result! I had used these before when I had been out on expeditions with the scouts, fantastic maps. Unfortunately the area I needed was covered over 2 separate maps and at £7.99 was a little pricey. I didn't have a lot of cash and what I had was really going to have to last me.

I did something I have never done before and slipped the 2 Southampton and area maps into my rucksack as stealthily as I could and moved on. The way I see it, it is not exactly like I am stealing everything. Let's face it these are desperate times. I'm not proud, but let's face it I have done a lot worse recently.

I walked around the shop and past the kids section; this is where I noticed the 'junior explorer' set, 'with working telescope and compass'. I figured that it would be a load of shit, but how badly can you make a compass? I mean, it's just a moving tiny magnet isn't it? Besides £6.99 was a bargain, I was expecting to pay a lot more for a compass!

That just left the batteries and the paper which I picked up on the way to the counter.

"You off on an adventure?" Smirked the spotty 18 year old lad behind the counter.
"Duke of Edinburgh trip. I have left all my stuff in the house." I replied. Pretty believable I thought.

£15.97, ouch! Which leaves me with a little under £10 to live on for the rest of my life!

I paid and turned to leave, immediately noticing the security gate. 'What if these maps are tagged?' I thought. I took off my rack sack which contained the booby trapped maps and approached. The gate was quite short and I am quite tall. As I walked up to the gate I winched the rucksack high into the air and jumped with it, just about clearing the top of the gate. Nothing, no noise.

As I stepped out of the shop and into the cold morning air, it caught my throat and reminded me just how crappy I was feeling. I had to get some pain killers and throat sweets. While I'm here I should get some food and water I thought too.

The high street had a chemist about 50 meters from where I was and a greengrocers just a little further down than that.

My shopping list:

- 1 packet of cheap ibuprofen
- 1 packet of blackberry flavor throat sweets – these are disgusting, I knew I should have bought the cherry flavored ones!
- One 1.5 litre bottle of water
- 3 oranges
- 3 apples
- 2 tins of spam – I am sure I like this!
- 1 packet of digestives
- 1 packet of frankfurters (on offer)
- 1 pack of 4 hot dog rolls (on offer)
- 1 packet of rich tea (broken and on offer)

- 2 rolls of toilet paper
- 1 small bottle of ketchup (what is life without its treats!)

This all came to £8.53, a lot of money but it should hopefully see me through a good few days. Only having a very small amount of money did really worry me, how could I get more? Stealing was an option I suppose, then I remembered the portable game in my rucksack and felt slightly better. I could always sell that.

It was time to get out of this town, so I knocked back 2 ibuprofen, put a throat sweet in, looked at my shite new compass and headed in the direction of what was hopefully south.

I reached the edge of the town around lunchtime, where I stopped and discovered that I really don't like Spam! I mean who could? It tasted like I was eating meat flavored with body odour! I then followed the B3355 south towards the M3 (obviously staying out of sight the whole time). It was getting late when I pitched my tent in a wooded area just outside a town called Chandler's Ford. The compass and maps have already proved their weight in gold. Stolen gold.

I decided to read the newspaper tomorrow, it has been a hectic day and I am too tired to deal with that now. Maybe I will feel better after a good night's sleep. I knocked back 2 more ibuprofen and fell asleep instantly.

## Monday, March 27th

I didn't sleep well at all last night. After having initially virtually passed out through sheer exhaustion, I woke up at around 3am. I must have spent about 2 hours dwelling on what was in the paper and creating my own versions of what it said and the pictures of me emblazoned throughout. I definitely should have read it before I tried to sleep, nonetheless, I continued to resist and lay there just thinking about it. When I eventually did fall asleep again I kept waking up to strange noises. I wish to god I had never seen that bloody Blair Witch Project now. I had the weirdest dream as well, not the hotel one. Something altogether weirder and infinitely more terrifying.

I dreamt that I was in a forest in the middle of summer. Sasha, Martin and my little brother were there and we could all jump really high, like super high – it was awesome, odd but awesome. I had also somehow managed to perfect this strange jumping technique and seemed to be able to pause myself in the air, while the others would fall straight back to Earth. The sky darkened all of a sudden with hazes of purple and grey and swirls of black and we stopped our jumping games and turned. A clattering sound, distant at first and ever growing started to come towards us. I jumped and paused and saw an army of skeleton type creatures about 5000 strong marching straight for us. Drums started up and horns rang out. The skeletons then started chanting "Kill! Kill!! Kill!!!" louder and louder and their pace quickened.

We started to jump away, I paused in the air occasionally to check on their progress, they were gaining on us, it didn't seem like we were going to get away. No matter how fast we went, they always seemed to faster.

"Kill! Kill!! Kill!!!" their voices were booming and increasing in speed and intensity, they were right behind us now. Martin tripped fell and his blood curdling scream rang out above their horrible chant, then he was gone.

They were right on us, I tried to pull my brother and Sasha to make us go faster. With the smell of rotting flesh in my nostrils a claw slashed across my back. A sickening warmth engulfed my back as blood poured from me. My brother screamed as a mutilated creature with the face of Todd tore through his throat with its razor sharp claws, in a tidal wave of blood he was gone.

In desperation I tried to jump, pulling with Sasha with me. I started going up, but stopped as the creatures grabbed her. She screamed and screamed as they literally ripped her to pieces. They pulled me to the ground, stopped and stood back.

Time stood still for a moment, the only sound to be heard was that of my heavy breathing. One of the skeletal Todd's moved forward and hissed at me, slowly pulling a knife from behind him using his thumb to skillfully swing it open.

My heart raced, I could not move. I was pinned down with pure fear.

He came closer and closer and started to lean towards my face.

As quick as a flash he lunged at me and the knife crunched straight through my left cheek bone with horrific force, up towards the back of my eye socket deforming my face as it went through. The pain was incredible and the sight in my left eye faded and disappeared.

I tried to scream but nothing came out.

He lunged with his empty left hand and caught me with his thumb straight into the corner of my right eye. His boney fingers wrapped themselves around the back of my head and he began to push.

Again I tried to scream, but I couldn't. I tried to move my arms but I couldn't.

My eye gave in to the pressure and yielded to his thumb. But his thumb carried on going. I was blind. His thumb reached the back of my eye socket.

He pulled the blade from my face. I took a deep breath and held it. I felt his knife crash down on the top of my head and I awoke.

A pretty mad dream, and I remember it vividly. I would like to have that one analysed. I know that the jumping must be significant, probably something to do with freedom, with me having more than everyone else. Losing my loved ones so viciously must surely be a reflection of what I'm experiencing. The rest is just a bit too mad.

I ventured out of the tent and the area was just woodland, with as far as I could make out no people or houses around for miles, a really great spot. I decided that I would stay put and rest for the day, after all I really hadn't slept well at all, still felt ill and that dream had really unsettled me.

I spent the day thinking, reflecting and planning. I have decided that the journey to France is not only doable but the best way forward for me. I cannot go on living like this. I will quickly run out of money, be seen or end up so ill that I will need to see a doctor or go to a hospital. In France I figure I can walk around pretty openly and maybe even work to earn a few quid if need be. If I stay the only real option for getting more money in the long term would be to turn to crime, I have already stolen a map and murdered someone, I'd like to think that was enough crime for one lifetime…..well, maybe one more.

I have decided that I am going to head to Southampton and scout out a boat at one of the marinas that I hope to find there (having never been to Southampton, I have no idea what is or isn't there!). I don't know an awful lot about boats, but the plan is to steal one at night and make the crossing to France. I have to be sure to select a tidy but not too expensive boat that hopefully won't be overly complicated and not too sorely missed.

I drew a line between Southampton and France on my map and roughly calculated that the distance I would need to travel is 109 miles (which doesn't seem too far, I was expecting that it would be more). I have no idea how fast boats go, but if I assume they go at about 30mph (I'm sure I should be writing that in knots, but have no idea how to convert it!). Travelling at that speed I have approximated that the journey should take me about 3.5 to 4 hours. There are obviously factors that need to be taken into consideration here: wind, currents, having enough fuel to make the crossing and what do I do if the worst comes to the worst and I miss/can't find France? I definitely need to buy a book about boats! A dummies guide is probably my best bet or maybe visit a library.

I finally plucked up the courage to read the newspaper, it sent a chill down my spine as I read it. I have tried my hardest to push the whole event in the lane out of my mind and reading the story brought it all flooding back. I turned to page 6. The faces of Todd and myself were staring straight back at me.

The story read:

*A 16 year old boy was found stabbed to death in an alleyway in Worthing on the evening of Friday 3$^{rd}$ March. The boy's blood soaked body was discovered* *by police who were alerted to the scene by his distressed friend. It is the latest in a long line of tragic stabbings along the south coast involving teenagers and this epidemic of violence is all too often related to gang disputes and drug dealing.*

*The victim has been named as Todd Phillips of Worthing (pictured above). He sustained a fatal stab wound to the neck, which punctured several major blood vessels which caused him to bleed to death. A friend of the deceased said of him "he was a popular lad in the area and will be sorely missed, I have no idea why someone would want to do something like this, it's unbelievable."*

*The police are keen to talk to Matthew Patterson (16) of Worthing (pictured left) who has gone missing since the incident. Anybody with any information as to his whereabouts should contact Worthing police station on 01903 822 622.*

This really is typical, I am now certain I have made the right decision, there is no way I would have come out of this in any way other than a murderer. The press have made Todd out as the victim and me as a cold blooded gang killer on the run; god knows what my parents and Sasha must be thinking about me, surely they can't believe the story? They know me far too well. I have decided that when (or if) I get to France I will try and get a message home, how I have no idea at the moment but I feel I need to let everyone know that I am ok and it will at least allow me to explain my side of the story.

I spend the rest of the day chillin'. Crosswords and Sudoku's from the 'newspaper' with a leaky old pen I found in the side pocket of the ruck sack have been a welcome distraction since reading the article. I played the console for a bit too, but the battery is getting a little on the low side now.

I have the adapter with me, but you don't get many power points in the countryside!

### Tuesday, March 28th

I managed to sleep pretty well last night, a day of not walking and relaxing has really recharged my batteries and I have made some really good progress today. The weather has started to feel a lot more like spring too which has also helped. The nights really have been painfully cold at times.

I left the vicinity of Chandlers Ford very early and crossed over the M3 before the morning commute started. I followed the motorway south until it met the M27 and tracked that East for a mile or so before sitting up on the bank of the motorway (out of view) until darkness fell to ensure I crossed it unseen. I have never crossed a motorway before, I suppose not many people actually have, so two in one day is quite impressive.

I set up camp in a small woods just north of Bassett Green road, very quiet and peaceful, full of trees and bushes in full bloom. The smell of new spring flowers and freshly cut grass was amazing and took me right back to sitting in my back garden playing swing ball with my little brother. It was definitely the nicest place I have pitched tent to date.

This stolen maps and shitty little kids compass are proving priceless. I know where I am, I know where I'm heading and I know where to avoid.

Considering I must have walked about 7 or 8 miles today, it's mad to think that I did not come across one single person today (other than those in cars). I am hoping that I will make it to Southampton tomorrow. There will undoubtedly be a lot of people between here and there and, a very real chance someone could recognise me from the recent picture in the paper, there may even have been a feature on the local news too. The plan for tomorrow is to head for a park just north of Woolston railway station. The map suggests that it is not very built up in that area. I am hoping that there will be somewhere nearby where I can crash down for a night or two undetected.

Tomorrow is going to a very big day.

My stomach is cart wheeling at the moment. I am unsure whether it is just nerves ahead of tomorrow or whether it is related to my recent piss poor diet. Whichever way you look at it I definitely need more toilet roll! Dear diary, out of courtesy I will spare you the details of my 'shitting arrangements,' let's just say it's disgusting and involves a complex combination of squatting, leaning and patience.

## Wednesday, March 29th

I bottled it today and did not get as far as I feel I should have, I left the safely of the woods just after 6:30 am and walked out onto Bassett Green road feeling pretty confident about the day. After about an hour of walking south the little surrounding suburbs of Southampton started to come alive with people on their way to work. No matter how you look at it, a teenage lad walking around a sleepy residential area with a huge rucksack and a carrier bag is out of place and draws attention. Maybe I am over reacting, but I am sure people were staring and doing 'double takes' to check what they had just seen. I started feeling less and less comfortable and just wanted to get out of view.

I altered my route slightly and crossed a river and entered Riverside Park. The park follows the river (obviously) south and I hugged the water to try and stay out of view of dog walkers and joggers. I reached the south most point of the park by 10am, back tracked into some dense bushes, found a small gap and climbed into my sleeping bag and laid low.

I spent an hour and a half playing Vista until the batteries run out and then had a nap.

I have decided to try and find a locker to leave my rucksack in, if I am going to be able to move around freely without having panic attacks I am going to have to blend in a lot more, today really shook me up and I am still not convinced that I have actually gotten away with it either, a lot of people saw me today.

Hopefully there will be some lockers at Woolston railway station, I will have to get up really early tomorrow to make the journey a little less stressful.

I have just been woken up (It's just gone 4:00am) because a fucking fox was pissing on my sleeping bag, it fucking stinks.

This is the first and last time I sleep rough!

## Thursday, March 30th

I walked out of Riverside Park at 5:16 stinking of fox piss. If I wasn't conspicuous before, well I certainly am now! Now you can smell me downwind from about 2km away. Brilliant.

I reached the train station just after 7:00 and it was thankfully empty. The walk there was not too bad, just a really lingering stare from an old lady walking her mangy little mutt, but I did my best to naturally obscure my face from her view.

Woolston station did have a locker section. I removed the Vista and map from my rucksack and then with a huge amount of effort managed to just about pack it into the tight space. From the station I walked towards the Itchen Bridge, which would take me down into the town. I noticed a launderette near the station and checked the closing time as I had no intention of sleeping in fox piss again.

I have never been to Southampton before; it's quite a nice town, certainly a lot better than Worthing. I found a Cash Converters shop on the outskirts and sold the Vista for £30.00 which, although not a lot, it is a lot better than nothing!

I definitely needed a shower, so I checked one of the information boards in the town centre, there was a swimming pool just over a kilometer away. I stopped at a pound shop and picked up a £1 towel, then a pit stop at Primark for a pair of swim shorts and headed off for the pool. Mud, sweat and fox piss was definitely gonna make me stand out in a crowd, I definitely needed a wash. The pool was very quiet, just a few old men and women doing their daily laps. I paid, changed, bought a small bottle of shower gel from the vending machine and showered. It's a good job no one was in the showers with me as the water coming off me was black. I swam gently for half an hour, the water felt great and I left the pool refreshed and ready for anything.

I headed back towards the town to try and find a book on boats, but stopped first in a café for a bacon sandwich and a cup of tea. I picked up one of the free papers and flicked mindlessly through. And then, there I was. Page 7, small photo of me in my school uniform from year 10 and a brief story. It read something along these lines:

### *Teen on the run*
*Worthing teen, Matthew Patterson (16) is still at large and wanted by police to help with their inquiries following the fatal stabbing of another teen. It is believed that Matthew is hiding out in or around the South Downs area to the north of Worthing. Police are conducting a comprehensive search of the area with tracker dogs, but so far have no strong leads. Phillip Ballard of Worthing police said "We are appealing to the local community to be vigilant and to contact us with any possible sightings of Matthew. It is very important that we speak with him in relation to the incident that took place on Friday 3rd March. We have evidence that leads us to believe that Matthew has head up into the South Downs and are working with other agencies and neighboring forces to ensure we apprehend him quickly and safely. Anyone with information should contact Worthing police station on 01903 822 622 as soon as possible."*

They are clearly on to me, but it certainly seems that I am one step ahead at the moment. I really do need to get a move on escaping the country though; it will only be a matter of time until they track me to here.

I bought my book about boats, writing paper, envelopes and some stamps from WH Smiths and head back to the locker to collect my sleeping bag for washing at the launderette. I had considered stealing the items from WH Smiths, but probably best not to push my luck at the moment.

I have settled down in a disused and dilapidated junction box just down the track from the station, it's like being in the Ritz! I have a freshly laundered sleeping bag and a book on boats that I can read by torch light. Luxury!

### Friday, March 31st

I woke up refreshed in my junction box paradise, albeit a little cold and frosty. I hid my kit behind a broken door and head off to look for a boat to steal.

I wrote 2 letters today, one to my parents and one to Sasha. I haven't decided on how I am going to get them posted without giving myself away, I did buy stamps but I'm not sure if that is the best way to do things. I'm pretty sure the postmark would give my current location away. I will have to think about it carefully.

Letter 1

*Dear Mum, Dad and Oliver*

*I know how much you must be worrying about me, I am ok. I am scared, lonely and not 100% sure what to do, but I'm ok.*

*I want you to believe me when I say that I never meant to hurt anyone, let alone kill. It was completely in self-defense. I am in hiding at the moment as I don't think the police will believe me because the only person who was there to witness what happened was Todd's friend.*

*Todd was waiting for me in a lane and he attacked me with a knife. I hit him and knocked the knife out of his hand. I grabbed the knife from the floor to stop him getting it back and he attacked me again. I swung the knife and the rest you know.*

*I can't take back what I have done, god knows I wish I could. I also can't take the punishment or blame for this, it just would not be fair. I am sorry for what has happened, no matter how much of an idiot he was, he did not deserve to die. I am so sorry for what has happened.*

*I have no idea what I am going to do. Maybe I will come home, maybe hand myself in, but at the moment I am not ready to do either. I am thinking a lot, that's all I can say at the moment.*

*I am sorry that this has happened; believe me when I say that I would like nothing more than to come home right now. But at the moment, I just cant. I love you all like mad.*

*I will write again soon*

*Love Matt*

Letter 2

*Dear Sasha*
*I miss you, I love you.*

*You must know that I did not do this on purpose.*

*Todd came at me with a knife in a lane and I knocked it out of his hands and picked it up. He came at me again and I stabbed him in self-defense. I wish to god I hadn't, I am not planning on coming home, at least not yet. I don't think the police will see things right and I fear that I will end up in jail over this, I don't think I could deal with that.*

*At the moment, I am free. Free to think. I am obviously very confused and really unsure of what to do for the best.*

*I am alone and very scared. I desperately want to see you again, but at the moment that would be impossible. Please keep this letter secret and safe (hoping you get it).*

*I don't even know whether you will receive this letter, but if you do could you place an online advert on eBay for the thing I stepped on when I came for dinner first. At least then I will know my letters can get through to you and we will take it from there.*

*Be in touch as soon as I can.*

*Love you with all my heart!*

*Matt*


Not my finest work granted, but I really just wanted to let everyone know I'm ok. I am quite pleased by the bit about 'Ebay. Kind of makes me feel like a private detective on a big case. I addressed them both and put them in my bag. I am serious about seeing Sasha again though diary. I have not got a clue how, or even if it will ever be possible. But this is a good start. I have seriously considered handing myself in and throwing myself at the mercy of the UK justice system just so I get to see her again.

I have read a lot about motor boats now and feel more confident about my extremely ambitious channel crossing. It is still my favored plan.

# April

## Saturday, April 1st

After a decent night's sleep in my dingy little junction box (the novelty has well and truly worn off already!) I woke up cold but with a plan.

The first train of the day arrived at just after 5:45am (as timetabled), the doors opened and I nipped into the sleepy carriage (I noticed 2 passengers in this section, both seemed half asleep and I don't think either of them noticed me) I popped my 2 'stamped and addressed' letters onto an empty seat and nipped back out again. A bit of a long shot I suppose, and a bit dodgy but worth the risk. Hopefully someone will have the decency to post my letters, and the postmark won't be Southampton so I figured that I would be less likely to give my location away.

After my daring letter posting mission I decided to wander to the coast and start to scout out a few boats and marinas and just get a general lay of the land. Woolston station is only about a 10 minute walk from the coast, I walked to the Itchen Bridge and turned left following the water flowing out to sea (logic dictated to me that that is where I would find boats!). The area to the left of the bridge was a rundown industrial area. I wandered through what was effectively a ghost town. I walked for about 2 miles and despite a few larger boats attached to buoys in the middle, this side of Southampton was pretty devoid of boats. I cut back on myself and head over the bridge to explore what was on the other side of the river.

I reached the other side of the bridge and turned left, again to follow the river south. This side was full of small tightly packed shitty little terraced houses and tightly packed cars. There were people everywhere! This was not a place I wanted to hang around I. As I reached the end of one street and looked to turn down a small lane, I noticed a woman who must have been in her 40's or 50's (hard to say around this area, as everyone just looked bloody weird). This woman just stared at me, just stood there and stared. Her friend, an equal aged chubby woman with a cigarette and a limp waddled out of the house and stood beside her staring mate and joined in staring at me.

"That's him" She said, then she shouted "That's fucking him!!"

My face lost colour and my legs felt weak, fuck fuck fuck I have been busted by the shittest crime fighting duo ever!!

I tried to act naturally, tried to style it out. I tried not to walk faster but my mind was racing.

I reached the corner of the road, my heart well and truly in my throat. They were still shouting as I disappeared out of their view and immediately broke into a sprint. I was certain that they would ring the police and I would not have long before they arrived. I sprint straight back over the bridge and then jogged the remainder back to my junction box collapsing with exhaustion once I have clambered inside.

A police siren.

Another police siren.

Yet another police siren, then nothing.

I was scared to move and to breathe. I had visions of police in legions, combing the streets with dogs while helicopters buzzed overhead scanning all derelict building for body heat.

One thing is very clear. I have to get out of here. I have to get out of here as soon as possible.

## Sunday, April 2nd

Needless to say I had a rotten night's sleep and I have not moved from here, I dare not even make a sound. There have been no noises from outside. The temperature has dropped making things very uncomfortable and to make matters worse I have been joined by a rat who seems to have taken up residence on the other side of the junction box in a hole in the wall.

I am so bored. I have decided that I will wait until darkness sets in and have another go at searching for boats/marinas.

With not a lot else to do I will settle down, keep warm and read the rest of my 'boat' book.


**Monday, April 3rd**
The midnight boat reconnaissance mission went well. I was not immediately rugby tackled on leaving the station and there were not hordes of police hunting the streets in packs for me.

In fact there was no one on the streets at all, it was far too cold for anyone with any sense to be out and about.

I walked back to the same street I was spotted on and continued to follow the river south. This area proved useless, after the residential area it became very industrial and the only boats along the waterfront were huge. I suppose they were not boats at all, but ships.

I doubled back on myself hugging the water as much as I could. I walked for miles until I saw it, 'Millbrook Sailing Club'. I was getting extremely cold so didn't spend a lot of time looking around. It was a small club with its own private marina and a small owners club on site. The site was secured with fencing and a gate, which didn't look as if it would be too tricky to negotiate. The boats were tricky to make out in the dark so I chanced a quick look with my torch, the majority of crafts were sailing boats, but a quick scan of the pontoons revealed a small number of motor boats including a couple of cabin cruisers. I had decided, this was where I was going to set out from. The only question that remained was when.

I wearily walked back to the junction box, where my rat flat mate and supper of 2 mars bars were waiting for me.

**Tuesday, April 4$^{th}$**
I have decided that I will leave for France tonight. It is early morning here in junction box paradise and I am busy
There are a two things I need to do before I leave.
1) Buy a couple of petrol tanks and fill them with petrol. The cabin cruisers do seem to be my best bet, the book I am reading does seem to suggest that they are pretty reliable, especially the types with an 'inboard' motor as opposed to an 'outboard'. This type of boat will provide me with decent cover, especially if the trip takes a while – truth be told I have not got a clue how long it will take or if it is even possible!
2) Find an internet café and check whether Sasha has advertised for a cat's tail!

I will sign off for now dear diary as there is a lot to do ahead of tonight. Wish me luck!

**Wednesday, April 5th**


**Thursday, April 6th**

I am sat on a beach in France (well at least I think so!), absolutely no idea where! It is currently 06:33am and I am absolutely freezing, but I'm here and in one piece.

I am curled up and resting in the boat halfway up a deserted and rocky beach. I managed to drag the boat up the beach a fair way, but had to stop as the rocks started to increase in size. The beach and its surrounding look stunning in the early dawn glow. It is just a small stretch of beach, almost like a cove surrounded on all sides by lush green hills that rise up away from the small jagged cliff line. I figured I would rest for a while and then try to pull the boat to the side of the beach and try to find a place to hide it, or at least make it a little more inconspicuous.

The journey across was very scary and I really don't think I would have done it had I known just what it was going to be like.

I packed up all my Earthly belongings and set off from the junction box just after 7 as it was starting to really become dark and head towards the town centre. A mile into my walk I chanced upon a petrol station

and bought a petrol can and filled it up with unleaded. As I walked on I reached the left hand turn that would take me down to the marina. I hid the full petrol can in a bush nearby and carried on walking towards the town. Another mile and I came across another petrol station, I again purchased a can and petrol and returned to stash it with the first. I walked on again, back past the petrol station and onwards towards the town, eyes peeled for an internet café. As I got closer to the centre the streets started to get busier and busier and I started to get more and more concerned about being identified. I had no choice, I had to carry everything with me. I could risk losing the petrol, but not all my things, it was a risk I had to take. I walked on with my face down and my eyes sweeping the ever increasing numbers of shops and businesses. Then I saw it, a job centre. I crossed the road to get a better look, it was open. The centre was filled with boards covered in postcards undoubtedly advertising a whole host of local positions which needed filling. All along the side of the centre were computers, a few of them being used by jobseekers. I entered the centre, sat at a computer and started to search eBay.
I looked over my shoulders, no one there, so I typed 'cats tail' and hit enter.

1 result. I clicked it with butterflies flooding through every blood vessel in my body.

It was Sasha. I eagerly read the advert she had created.
'For sale, one cat's tail – see photos attached for more details'.

I clicked the photos, the first one was as the advert dictated – a picture of a cat's tail. The second was a picture of the coffee table in her house, there was a note on it. I zoomed in.
It read:

*'Dear Matt,*
*I love you and know you didn't kill Todd on purpose, I know it was an accident. We all know it was an accident. We all miss you so much, most of all me. I ache for you. I have created a new email address that I will only access from school so nobody traces it, we can stay in contact that way.*
*bowlingqueen@hotmail.com I will check it every day.*
*Love*
*Sasha*
*XXX*

Tears filled my eyes, I felt warm all over and so happy. I checked over my shoulders again, still no one near me so I turned back to the computer and got to work.

I created my own new email account bowlingjoke@hotmail.com and wrote Sasha a brief message.

*Dear Sasha*
*Words cannot explain how happy I am right now. You are so clever! I am in Southampton at the moment typing this from a job centre. I am just about*

*to cross the channel to France – I will explain how another time!*

*I must see you. I don't know when I will have access to email again. Not for a little while for sure, so here is the plan. I will meet you on Saturday April 17$^{th}$ at 9:00pm by the ticket barriers to the international train at Paris, Gare du Nord.*

*What we will do when we meet, I don't know. Maybe I will when I see you.*

*I love you with all my heart.*

*Matt*
*XXX*
*P.S. Delete the eBay advert!*

I left the Job centre with a new found spring in my step and a drunken smile on my face and set off to retrieve my hidden petrol cans and headed towards the marina.

The marina was deserted when I arrived apart from some sort of small function going on in the boat owners club. When I arrived there were a couple of people smoking outside and talking far too loud. I waited until they went back in and slipped silently inside the open gates. I hugged the shadows on the far side of the yard, arrived at the pontoon and threw my bag and petrol cans (carefully onto the bag so as not to make too much noise) over the tiny security gate, checked around one final time and then quietly climbed over myself. I walked to the end of the pontoon where I started examining the cabin cruisers moored there. There were 6 in total, all fairly small but they were all tidy and looked up to the task ahead. I looked around the first but noticed the heavy duty clamp attached to the wheel, a definite no, I moved on. I looked around the others and made a decision. The boat was perfect, obviously used for day fishing trips as it had a good supply of nets, rods and reels in the cabin and a fish finder by the wheel, but was low on security. Like the others I have looked over this boat needed a key to start it, but I figured that it would be quite straight forward to 'hot wire'. How hard could that be? I returned to a few of the other boats and retrieved a few additional items: a life jacket, some oars, a length of rope and a couple of half empty cans of petrol with a spare pump. I untied the boat, grabbed one of the oars and pushed off from the side of the pontoon, I was away. The wobbling made my already nervy stomach turn over and I felt as if I was going to vomit. Rowing was very difficult; the boat was small, but clearly not designed for this kind of propulsion, except in an absolute emergency obviously. The oars barely touched the water, and due to the width of the boat I was having to row on one side then move to the other, each time having to lean over the side to get the oar deep enough in the water, it was really not easy going at all.

I caught a glimpse of a figure with a torch walking through the marina and froze solid. I didn't account for any security guards at a little marina like this and no idea what I would do if I was spotted. The figure walked up to the gate that I had scaled just 5 minutes ago and paused, my heart was racing. I heard the gate rattle, the torch flicked around the pontoon and then away. The figure walked past the gate and back up the path towards the club where I could still hear the faint sound of music and drunken laughter. Close one, it must have been a security guard doing his rounds, luckily for me in a very half arsed manner!

I rowed slowly out of the marina gateway and out to sea, the muscles in my arms were aching. It must have taken me about 30 minutes of continued hard effort to get this far, but I dared not attempt to start the motor just yet. The water was calm but the current kept pushing me back towards the marina, progress was painfully slow. After another 10 minutes I decided that I would have to start the motor, I had nothing left to give and I was certainly far enough away for the sound not to cause alarm.

I recalled all I read from my little boat book. I turned the fuel tap open and pumped the bulb to get the fuel to the engine and then turned my attention to the ignition. Using the handle end of an oar I provided the barrel with a couple of accurate whacks and it fell apart. I explored the remains and started to pull the wires apart. I located the live and began stroking it against the others. The engine burst into life with an amazing amount of noise. I tied the two wires together and I was away, I turned the throttle down to reduce the noise from the motor, looked at the compass, lined the boat up and set off.

In all the adrenaline fuel activity I hadn't realized just how cold it was and now being in the open water with no cover on either side I was really starting to struggle. I put on a few more layers and the life jacket, but just could not get warm. There was no way I would last half hour, let alone make it all the way to France in this blistering cold. Then I had a great idea. I located the rope and fastened it across the top of the wheel then guided one side through the door of the cabin and the other though the window. I got into the cabin shut the door and window as much as I could and tried my new invention. It was crude, but worked well enough. I placed the map and compass of the table, covered myself in the nets and began to relax a little.

All was going pretty well, I was heading south out of Southampton towards the Solent, the banks either side pulling ever further and further away and then the engine stopped. It was silent. I untangled myself from the nets and headed to the back of the boat. No petrol. In my eagerness to get away I had neglected to check just how much fuel I had in the tank. I refilled the tank, pumped the fuel bulb and restarted the engine.

The next few hours passed without incident. I negotiated the Solent passing around the East side of The Isle of Wight and the headed out to sea. It was then that the waves started.

The temperature dropped further, the wind picked up and at this point I really thought things were going to end very badly indeed. The little boat was being thrown around, the sea felt as if it was just dropping away like I was on a rollercoaster and it wasn't long before I was throwing up like a good un. I opened up the throttle as much as possible and ploughed my way through, it really felt like I was going to capsize at any moment. I endured about an hour and a half of these torrid condition before the sea showed mercy and let me pass in peace.

Another hour of pretty calm seas and I checked the petrol and topped it up and settle down to eat a little to replace the several litres of sick I had fired out of my guts.

Two more hours or so of reasonably calm seas and the distant lights of France had me in floods of tears and uncontrollable laughter. I allowed myself to relax.

I woke up with a jump. It was a little after 7 in the morning and I was lost. Panic hit me, nothing in any direction apart from sea. I had no idea at all where I was and the engine had stopped. I stepped out onto the deck and checked the wind, then the compass. The wind was blowing strongly from the East, my best guess was that I had been blown to the west and that I should do my best to head South East to hit land. I filled up the tank, (I was now down to my final can) and restarted the engine and set off. I travelled South East for a little over 4 and a half hours and saw nothing. The engine stopped and I refilled it with my final can. The wind was still blowing quite hard, but I decided to do my best to stay put and wait until darkness fell to give me the best chance of spotting land. I searched the little boat and located the anchor. It was a small anchor, that was probably only useful when in shallow waters, but it was all I had so I threw it over board and hoped for the best. I let out the anchor line and ran out, the anchor was still not down. I undid the rope from the wheel and attached that and continued to let it out, still not down. My last option was to use the nets. I gathered them up from the cabin and did my best to unravel them to get the most length out of them. I estimated I had created another 20 meters, but that was all. I attached it to the anchor line and began to let it out slowly. Down, down, down……..touchdown!

I retreated into the cabin, curled up and waited until darkness fell.
I bobbed around what I hoped was still the English Channel for hours. It started to get dark a little after 7, but I sat tight for another 2 boring hours until it was pitch black to give me the maximum chance of seeing light. At this stage I didn't care if I ended up back in England. Better that than die at sea. And, a crap sea too, the bloody English Channel, not the Pacific or Atlantic Ocean! Not even a sea!!

I clambered out of my reasonably sheltered cabin and into the frosty night. The sea was dead calm. I pulled up the anchor, restarted the motor, pointed the boat South East and opened the throttle to half way, I figured that a steady pace was the best option to conserve what little fuel I had left.

An hour into my journey my heart leapt with joy as a tiny speck of light appeared on the horizon. I readjusted the direction of the boat and headed straight for it.

Within just 10 minutes I could make out that the light was coming from a large ship that was clearly coming towards me. I adjusted my direction to avoid a head on collision and so as not to be spotted. In just a few moments I was passing by the side of a huge ferry, it was lit up pretty well and I scanned the sides for any clue as to where it was coming from or heading, then I saw it. Southampton – St Malo. I quickly checked the map and then head off in the wash of the Southampton bound ferry. Within the hour the tiny flicker of lights began appearing in front of me, I opened up the throttle and head towards them.

Another half an hour passed and I started to make out the shapes of buildings illuminated dimly by the yellow glow of the approaching streetlights. I could now see the coast line and reduced the throttle and started to follow it in an attempt at finding a quiet spot to moor up the boat. After 10 minutes or so the lights on the land started to disappear, this was perfect. The engine stopped, not so perfect!

I quickly rushed to the back of the boat and examined the tank, completely empty. I picked up the oar and started to row. It was no use, no matter how hard I tried I was constantly being forced back, the tide must have been going out. I persevered for about 2 hours before exhaustion forced me to stop. I sat breathing heavily as the boat gently started bobbing away from the coast. I decided at that point that diving over the side and swimming for it would probably be the best option, but it was so cold that I figured that attempting it now would be suicide, best to wait until the sun has had a chance to warm the water up a little. I dropped the anchor and retreated into my cabin to wait for the day to start.

I dozed for a while and tried to put the impending icy swim out of my mind. I was jolted awake and jumped up. The sun was rising and I could see the coast quite clearly and I could also see that the anchor line was straining in the direction of it. I pulled up the anchor, grabbed an oar and began paddling again. This time with greater success.

Half an hour of paddling and being dragged around by the strong currents of the rocky coast line I saw the beach and doubled my efforts. Closer, closer, closer…..land.

I dragged the boat up the beach, I had made it.


### Friday, April 7$^{th}$

After dragging the boat at the base of the cliff at the East side of the beach I allowed myself to relax a little. The beach was deserted. There were no clear paths, no houses or roads in view so I made the cabin as cozy as I could and slept all day and all night, I was exhausted mentally and physically.

After waking this morning I spent the day teaching myself to fish with mixed results. I have been fishing a couple of times before but only ever caught a few tiddlers. I figured that as I had all the kit, I would give it a go. I am pretty much out of food and only have a small amount of money left and that is in pounds too which is useless here.

I set up the 2 rods I found and baited 1 with limpets and the other with little snails I found on some of the rocks (I think they are periwinkles). Nothing! I wasted about 3 hours with these particular offerings and the only interest I received was from rather small unappetising crabs.

Next on the menu was a jellyfish I found washed up and a bunch of tiny shrimp like creatures I found in a rock pool which made the hook look a little like a wriggly fishy shish kebab. Success! Well, from the kebab, the jellyfish didn't even attract the crabs. Over a 2 hour period I caught 2 reasonably sized sea bass and that was it for the day. Only trouble is that I don't have any means of starting a fire to cook them. I suppose I could eat them raw, but I'm not that desperate just yet.

I settled down for the night in the cabin. Tomorrow I would explore the area.

## Saturday, April 8th

I woke up just after 6 very refreshed, but very hungry. I walked to the top of the beach and began tracking the cliff line for an easy route up. It was not particularly high, but I am certainly no climber. I found a section with a gentler slope upwards and some good foot and hand holds and began my ascent. I got to half way and the adrenaline began to flow. I stupidly looked down and made matters worse, I was frozen stiff and unsure what to do. I must have remained fastened to the rock face for at least 10 minutes panicking. Then, common sense swept through me along with the new found fighting spirit I seem to have developed and up I went.

I reached the top and pulled myself up and into a dense forest. I walked directly away from the beach, leaving the occasional stick stuck in the ground to help find my way back. After 30 minutes of walking I reached a break in the forest and walked out and into a small but empty car park. The car park joined a small road, across from which stood two small shops, I walked closer to investigate.

One was a fishmonger and the other a bakery. I crossed the road to take a closer look. I was looking through the fishmonger's window at the different fishes for sale and noticed the sea bass. 12 euros per kilogram for whole fish!! And 21 euros per kilogram of fillets!!! That was enough of an invitation for me, I went inside.

There was nobody around, the shop was small and clean, whoever owned it really did take pride in their work. I coughed to gain the owners attention and it had the desired effect. A man in his mid-fifties walked out from the backroom still drinking a cup of coffee. He was quite fat and very untidy with a good few day's growth of grey stubble on his chin. As I speak no French whatsoever and the man clearly spoke no English, our 'conversation' was comical.

As I left the shop we shook hands and smiled at each other. I think, we had just agreed that I would bring him sea bass and he would give me money......

I did manage to communicate to him that I needed a lighter and some water, he obliged and I returned to the beach with my bounty.

I spent the rest of the day fishing with my little shrimp kebabs and in the evening I lit a small fire and cooked the 2 bass I caught yesterday. I stored the further 8 I caught today in my rucksack to hopefully sell in the morning.

### Sunday, April 9th

I woke up early and headed back to the fishmongers with my 8 bass. The shop was closed when I arrived (I had forgotten it was a Sunday), I looked around the back and found a door, knocked gently and waited patiently in the cold morning air.

The untidy man opened the door and greeted me with a strong hand shake and a warm smile. I took out the fish and handed them to him. The expression on his face confirmed that he was happy and he disappeared inside with them. I waited excitedly for just a few moments and he returned with a crisp 20 euro note for me. We shook hands again and I went on my way.

I returned to the boat and got back to work. 5 bass today, 4 to sell in the morning, 1 for me.

After fishing I set about camouflaging the boat the best I could with all of the bits of wood and leaves I could find. It was a very quiet beach and I had not seen a soul since arriving, but I figured that blending the boat into the landscape would be wise, just in case. It wasn't a perfect job by any stretch of the imagination, you could still tell there was a boat on the beach, but it no longer looked out of place.

I decided that tomorrow I would wake up early and do a little more fishing before heading up to the shop. I would also take my map with me to see if I could figure out where I was and just how I can get to Paris.

**Monday, April 10$^{th}$**

I awoke at 5:30, set up the 2 rods and settled down to eat my breakfast of last night's bass. I promised myself there and then that I would stock up in the bakery if it was open as I am already getting very sick of eating barbequed fish!

I caught 1 more bass and 2 colourful fish which I had never seen before. I took them anyway, maybe they would be worth a couple of quid too.

I packed up the fish and the map, had a quick but breathtakingly cold wash in the sea and head off to the shop. I reached the shop a little after 10:00 am and was delighted to see that the bakery was indeed open. I walked into the fishmongers and was welcomed by my new friend. I pulled the fish out of the bag, he looked at the bass, smiled and laid them to one side. He took the 2 colourful fish behind the counter and dropped them straight into the bin and said, "Merde!" I knew what that meant.

"Café?" He asked. "Oui" I replied, he disappeared out the back and returned with a cup of coffee, croissant and 15 euros for the fish. I thanked him and sat in the seat he pulled out for me. I pulled out my map and with a series of points and shrugs managed to ask him where we were. He looked at the map for a few moments, shoved the last bite of croissant into his mouth and pointed. It appeared I had travelled a little further from St Malo than I thought and was just along the coast from a little town called Saint – Lunaire. There seemed to be plenty of roads, in the area, which made me think it would be pretty straight forward getting to Paris. By using my fingers as legs on the map and repeating the word 'Paris' while pointing at myself I think I managed to ask him how to get there.

He pointed at Saint – Lunaire and in very basic French (so I could understand) managed to explain to me that I needed to catch 3 busses. One from Saint – Lunaire into St Malo, another from St Malo to Rennes and a final one to Paris. He seemed to think that it would take about 5 or 6 hours to do the trip.

I sat and relaxed with him in the shop for a few hours. We drank coffee, ate cheese and bread and just sat in silence enjoying each other's company which was only interrupted when a customer came in, which wasn't often, business did seem slow. I guessed he lived alone, but couldn't be sure.

I left the fishmongers and visited the bakery to pick up some bread and a few pastries and returned to my little boat with a full stomach and a plan.

## Tuesday, April 11th

The 17th is fast approaching. I wonder if Sasha will make it. I worry that it was not Sasha and I have set myself a trap. The 17th is Sasha's birthday (which is why I picked it). I hope she doesn't mind my not getting her a present, I hope that I am enough.

**Wednesday, April 12th**

**Thursday, April 13th**

**Wednesday, April 14th**

**Thursday, April 15th**

**Friday, April 16th**

Dear Diary, apologies for my break in communication I am sat on my bed in a hotel room in Saint – Lunaire writing this. I have spent the last few days just catching fish and sitting in the fishmongers not speaking with my new best friend.

I left my boat this morning with a heavy feeling in my heart. I had really grown to love it. It had served me so well, it had gotten me across the English Channel and been my home for the last week or so. I hope someone else finds it and loves it as much as I did. I popped in on my friend and gave him a final goodbye handshake and set off on my 20 mile cross country trek to Saint – Lunaire.

I arrived in Saint – Lunaire at around 2pm, located the bus station and bought my tickets for Paris, I have to catch 3 busses tomorrow. The first leaves Saint – Lunaire at 9:15 and arrives in St Malo at 9:50. From St Malo then I catch the 10:30 bus to Rennes, which arrives at 11:40. My final bus leaves Rennes at 12:30 and gets into Paris, Gare du Nord at 4:30pm. This gives me plenty of time and allows for any potential problems.

With my tickets purchased, I scouted the town for the cheapest hotel I could find, and here I am.

Must dash as I am about to have the longest shower in the history of personal hygiene to get rid of the stink of fish which seems to have lodged itself in every single pore of my body.

Jail or Sasha? Either way I will be ready, clean and smelling nice.

### Saturday, April 17th

I leapt out of bus number 3 with a completely numb arse and dead legs and walked as fast as I could towards the train station without running so as not to arouse any suspicion. I reached the station entrance and looked in, it was busy. Really busy!

Buses truly are the most unreliable bloody things!! The first 2 buses were like clockwork, but the 3rd was cancelled. I sat in the bus station listening to a tannoy system giving useless information about god know what for 4 hours. I really am going to have to learn some French, I wish to god I had paid more attention in Mdm Jones's classes instead of just lusting after her giant baps! 4 hours late, surely that even rivals the British rail system!

The time was 8:47pm, I had made it and I was actually a little early too. There were police dotted strategically around the great open space of the stations main hall, I skillfully negotiated my way through them as I walked deeper and deeper into the station (just in case).

I could see the ticket barrier in the distance, my heart started to race. Adrenalin rushed around by body. If this was going to be a trap, so be it. If I was going to be truncheoned on the back of the head and carted off to jail, so be it. There was a chance that I may see her again. In short, I would die for that.

I stopped dead.

She was there. She ran to me, I ran to her.

We kissed, we cried.

I have Sasha.

I have hope.

Printed in Great Britain
by Amazon.co.uk, Ltd.,
Marston Gate.